COLLECTED SCIENCE FICTION SHORT STORIES: VOLUME ONE

A SHORT STORY COLLECTION

RAYMOND S FLEX

CONTENTS

SUITE PEACE

1

LEAVES BLEW into Jon's face. He held up his arm to shield himself then clutched his briefcase tighter and paced on. The hotel loomed ahead. Bags tugged at his lower eyelids. His mind was frayed and torn. Ten years he had been at this job, constantly on the move. If he had his way, this would be his last assignment. The problem was that his superiors would be the ones to decide. He sighed and pushed his way through a revolving door.

Heat billowed about the hotel reception. A few seconds later, his chills were replaced by sweats. He tugged his scarf loose and set his briefcase down at his feet. There was no sign of a receptionist. This place was a drone hotel, a design where, all going well, he would never see its employees. A computer terminal radiated blue light across the white tiles. He picked up his briefcase and approached.

A yellow smiley face appeared on the screen along with the message: 'Welcome to Ivory Tower Guesthouse. Please place your finger on the scanner to continue.' He did so and, after a brief pause, the machine *booped*. A churning sound followed from within the machine and a plastic card clattered into a metal tray. He pushed back the transparent plastic flap and retrieved it. Room 56. A drowsy feeling set in. He yawned, stretched then headed off down the hall, following the sign which read: Rooms 1 – 100.

His footfall hung in the empty corridor a second before the walls absorbed it. Shivers ran down his spine. The quiet and loneliness. He was so tired of it. His mind brought back images of his wife and two daughters. A hot sunny day, years ago now. It was that shred of memory which kept him going, in and out of these anonymous hotel rooms, day after day. Proof there was some light at the end of the tunnel. That and the logs: his life.

When he arrived outside Room 56, he glanced up and down the corridor then swiped his card and entered. Inside there was a king-sized bed and a large en suite bathroom. Netted curtains filtered grey daylight. A TV screen took up most of one wall, while a desk occupied another. A tingle ran through his veins. This was much nicer than the places Big Boss usually sent him. On the desk was a cardboard notice. He laid his briefcase down on a luggage rack and padded over. It was written in careful handwriting, blue ink:

Dear Mr Clifton,

Due to a technical issue, your room has been upgraded.
We appreciate your custom and hope you enjoy your stay.

Sincerely,

Margaret Manley
Customer Service

In all his years on the job, he had only received a handful of room upgrades. Some luck for once. He allowed the tension to seep from his shoulders then set about skimming the room for bugs.

Finding nothing out of the ordinary, he ended his search and flipped open his briefcase. His change of clothes: a white shirt, a pair of chino trousers, cotton briefs and a pair of white socks, padded his laptop which rested in the middle. He slid out the laptop, placed it on the desk and flipped it open, tapping the power button on the side. Listening to the familiar start up *hum*, he reached out and flicked the TV to a twenty-four hour news channel to keep him company.

Once he had signed himself into the internet with the company membership, he opened the database and set up the log-checking program. It was his job to keep watch on the logs for unauthorised access. He noticed a kettle at his elbow and he perused the options in the tray: two sachets of green tea, two hot chocolate and two sachets of coffee—one decaffeinated, the other caffeinated. It always amazed him that people actually drank decaffeinated coffee, what was the point? He tore open the caffeinated sachet, tipped its contents into a plastic cup then disposed of the foil wrapper in the bin.

After he'd drunk a cup of coffee, he lamented the fact he wouldn't be able to get another until his next hotel. No cleaning service allowed during a stay. There was no new activity on the logs, so he located a laundry bag at the back of his wardrobe, got undressed and put all his clothing in the bag, ticking 'Early Morning Express Service' on the form.

Naked, he cracked open the door and placed the bag outside. He showered then put on a fresh pair of underwear, set the logs to 'Alert Mode,' so any unauthorised access would trigger an alarm, then he slid in between the sheets and allowed himself to drift off to sleep. His dreams were the same as always. Hot summer day in the garden. Sipping a glass of wine with his wife. His daughters playing in the sandpit.

2

SOMETHING CLUNKED outside the door. His blood fizzed and he readied himself for attack. But none came. Light poured in through the curtains. He opened his eyes and rose to his elbows, squinted at the fresh blue sky then glanced at the alarm clock beside his bed. Seven thirty. He prised himself from his bed and padded across the room. With his eye to the spyhole, he looked out into the corridor. There, at the foot of his door, was a plastic bag and a tray covered in tinfoil. He unlatched the door then pulled the two items into the room.

The plastic bag contained his laundered clothes. He peeled back the tinfoil to reveal his breakfast: a serving of orange juice, a bowl of cereal and a banana. After putting his clothes to one side, he flipped on the TV and ate. When he finished, he took a shower, checked the logs then snapped his laptop shut and returned it to the briefcase. Checking his watch, he saw that he was on time for his meeting that morning. He scanned the room a final time then left, hanging the 'Do Not Disturb' sign on the handle.

3

THAT EVENING Jon returned to the hotel. He paced through the phantom reception. Although the clock on the wall read five thirty, it could've easily been midnight. Back in his room, he went through the usual routine, checking for bugs. When he reached the desk, he hung his jacket over the back of the chair and slipped his laptop out, powered on. Then he noticed the bin. It was empty. Someone had been in the room.

His heart tickled his throat. He ground his teeth and considered his next move. Last night he had drunk a cup of coffee and chucked the sachet into the bin. He was sure. On occasions like this, finding anything strange about the room, the procedure was to call Big Boss before taking any rash actions. First, though, he had to take care of the logs. He cancelled the internet connection on his computer and sat back to think.

There was no mistake. It made no sense. If the cleaner had come into the room why hadn't she bothered to hoover up? No, this was something sinister. A plot. He pulled his briefcase onto his lap and unzipped the hidden pocket in the lining to withdraw his mobile. Hands shaking, he punched in Big Boss's number. Almost of itself, his finger tapped the screen. He held the phone to his ear. It clicked. "Hello?" Jon said.

There was a bout of heavy breathing.

His stomach sank. He really was coming apart at the seams. How could he forget the procedure? Keeping the phone crooked between ear and shoulder, his fingers flew over the laptop keys, bringing up the encrypted password program. He entered the required data and read off the code.

A long pause on the other end then, "What's the trouble?"

"Someone's been in the room."

"Evidence?"

"Bin's been emptied."

"Clifton? Jon Clifton, is it?"

"That's right."

"How're the logs doing?"

Jon steadied his breathing. Sweat dampened his ear. He switched the phone to the other one. "I disconnected."

"Go back online and check."

Jon did as he was told. "Everything looks normal."

"Good. Listen, everything's probably fine. You've got to stay calm. Maybe the cleaning lady walked in without seeing the notice, cleared out the bin and then her superior called her out. It's no big deal, all right?"

Big Boss's words didn't do much to dampen Jon's paranoia. It was easy for him, God-knew-where, in some safe house. Sometimes he doubted his employer's commitment to the project.

"Was there anything else?"

Now was his opportunity. Maybe they would release him if he asked nicely. Jon traced a finger around his laptop case, leaving a thin trail of perspiration.

"No?"

"That was it."

The line buzzed then went dead.

He laid the mobile down alongside his laptop and continued to stare at it, as if it might jump up and rip out his throat. After a few seconds, he checked out the numbers dancing across the laptop screen. Nothing out of the ordinary.

A *crack* came from the corridor, followed by the *squeak* of wheels. He spun around. A shadow passed across the light at the base of the door. If Big Boss didn't recognise the danger, he did. He slapped his laptop closed, bolted across the room then ripped open the door.

A young woman stood behind a cart packed full with bottles of cleaning fluid. Rags stuffed into the upper compartment. Her eyes fixed onto his but her mouth remained a slit. "Is everything all right, sir?"

"What're you doing?"

"My job."

Jon peeled back his shirt sleeve and examined his watch. "Strange time, don't you think?"

She shrugged. "Guests come and go at all hours."

"Someone's been in my room, snooping about."

A smile turned the corners of her mouth. She nodded at his 'Do Not Disturb' sign. "Not if you've got that there, sir."

"Yeah? And what part of that didn't you understand?"

She sighed then made to push the cart on down the hall. "I just got here, just started my shift."

His chest prickled and blotches appeared in his vision. He reached out and grabbed hold of her wrist.

"Let go of me!" she said, attempting to shrug out of his grasp.

He leant over the cart and caught sight of a clipboard, a printout attached to it. "What's that?"

"Cleaning rota."

"Who was on this morning?"

She jerked again, pulling herself free this time, and continued on down the hall at double pace. "None of your business."

His heart fluttered. He had to reel himself in. It was important not to make a spectacle. They might be watching. But his work was his life. If he didn't protect it what did he have left? His throat felt dry and he could hardly get out the words. "S—sorry."

The cleaner disappeared around the corner.

He retreated into his room where he slumped in his chair, allowing the constant flow of numbers back and forth on his laptop screen to worm in and out of his brain. Why had he blown up? He supposed he hated people lying to him. Why couldn't those lowlifes just admit they'd entered his room? His mind spun. Maybe it had been the right thing to do—confronting the cleaning lady. If anyone had been watching they'd know he'd meant business. He smirked at that thought. Sure, attacking a defenceless woman. It brought him back to the real truth. He was burnt out.

Later that evening, while he was shaving, there was a series of *thuds* at the door. He dropped his razor in the sink and wrapped a towel around his waist. On the point of opening the door, he paused and peered through the spyhole. A small man dressed in a grey suit. He wore a silver name tag that glinted in the bright corridor lights. The words on it read: 'Night Manager.'

What had Jon done? He backed up and considered pretending to be out.

But then there was another knock on the door followed by a husky voice. "Sir, if you don't open the door, I'm calling the police."

Sparks seared his nerves. He had completely ruined whatever attempt he'd made at a low profile. "Coming." He waited a couple of seconds then opened the door.

The night manager cocked his head and squinted. "Mr Clifton?"

"Yes."

"We've had a report about you harassing a member of staff."

It was better to stay silent, apologise, then slink away tomorrow morning.

"I've just come to remind you that we won't tolerate such treatment."

"No, of course not."

"And to suggest that you act in a more gentlemanly manner in the future."

Heat rose in Jon's cheeks. This wasn't him. He was a normal, restrained man. It was just that this whole job had turned against him. He was sick and tired.

The night manager edged closer. "Any more behaviour like that and I'll have to ask you to leave."

Jon forced himself to smile. "Yes, I completely understand."

He turned away. "No matter who your employer is."

A shiver ran through Jon's bones. Forgetting he only wore a towel, he stepped out into the corridor. "What do you mean?"

The night manager smirked then continued on up the corridor.

Jon fought against every urge in his body not to go after him and demand an answer. He had already caused so much suspicion around his situation in the hotel. The man had called him out straight, his cover was blown. Only one thought struck him now: *Get out.*

He slipped back into his room, got dressed and packed. Once finished, he picked up his mobile and dialled up Big Boss. It rang a long time before he answered. He went through the password routine then said, "They know who I am, who I'm working with. I'm leaving."

"Not so fast."

"They might be coming at any second, for the laptop. The whole project will be blown."

"I'm sure it's all just in your mind—"

"No, the night manager knows. He said he knows who my employer is."

"Rubbish. If he did know, why would he tell you something like that?"

This shred of logic stopped Jon in his tracks. The way Big Boss said it seemed so matter-of-fact. That very simplicity made Jon believe that it couldn't be the correct solution.

"Listen to me. Have a cigarette, smoke some weed, whatever

you need to get your brain in gear and stop worrying. We'll move you on tomorrow."

Those words rattled about his brain. He had heard them so many times. *We'll move you on tomorrow.* At first they had meant comfort: a fresh start, but now he knew it meant the next step in a perennial cycle and he knew he could no longer dedicate himself to the project. His passion was dead. He thought of his wife and two daughters. Their smiles sent warmth slapping about his chest. He took a deep breath, closed his eyes and said, "I can't take it anymore. I want to retire."

"Are you sure?"

Those images of his wife and daughters lingered on his mind. "Yes."

Big Boss sighed then muttered to someone in the background. "I can trust you to see out the night without any more drama, can't I, Clifton?"

"Yes."

"Good, check the logs. Get some sleep. I'll have your replacement pick you up tomorrow at nine thirty. He'll take the laptop."

"Thank you."

"Clifton?"

"Yes?"

"It's been a pleasure working with you."

He would be free after tonight. A smile sprung up on Jon's lips. "I feel the same."

The line went dead.

4

IN THE MORNING Jon dressed and packed up. No unusual activity on the logs, so he shut down the laptop for the final time. At nine thirty there was a curt knock at the door. He opened up. A man stood there, back arched and eyes fixed on Jon's chest. He wore a black suit, shirt, tie and a pair of leather gloves. With a nod, he set off down the hall. Jon followed.

The man led him through the reception and out of the hotel. They continued up the road, winding up a hill, away from the city which sprawled out below. When the man got to the top, he led Jon down a narrow street and out to an empty lot. Grass grew between cracks in paving slabs. A burnt out house, three roofless walls, hid the area from view. The man pointed at the briefcase in Jon's hand. "Laptop in there?"

Jon nodded and handed it over.

The man bounced the briefcase in his hand, checking its weight, then laid it at his feet. He took a lungful of air then reached inside his jacket, produced a pistol and checked it over. Once satisfied, he nodded.

Blood pounded to Jon's temples. Soon he would be joining his wife and daughters. He thought of that one perfect summer afternoon, allowed it to carry his mind far away, over the trees. Somewhere, at the back of his consciousness, there was a *click* and a *snap*. His mind swam then faded into nothing.

SHALLOW ECHOES OF A
DYING STAR

1

HEINRICK TILTED the control stick away from him, keeping his eyes locked on the screen. Neon green gridlines were superimposed onto the vast emptiness of space, giving meaning to the otherwise ink-blot black. He kept the ship steady, steering through the markers—going along the route which had been planned out for him at Beta Command Post. All being well he would get there soon. Just a little further and then he could turn right round and go back home again.

His co-pilot, Roger, slept with his head resting against one of the windows looking out into the blackness of space. Drool bubbled at the corner of his mouth and he twitched every couple of minutes. Heinrick would let him sleep on for a little longer. It wasn't like there was any great action Roger was missing out on.

Heinrick, himself, found his head bobbing as he struggled to keep the stick straight. Normally he would have been able to leave the ship to the whim of the autopilot, but that had busted a light-year out from Beta, and Heinrick had had no intention of returning there—most likely they didn't even have the parts he needed anyway. He steered the ship through green square after green square, doing his best not to fall asleep.

Roger jerked in his sleep and then crooked an eye open. He spoke through a yawn. "You should've woken me, sir."

Heinrick smirked. "It's just that you looked so cute there, napping along like a baby."

"I was just tired, that's all."

"You wanna take over for a bit?" Heinrick said, leaning away from the control stick.

"Sure, captain."

When Heinrick released the control stick he saw that it had

impressed its form on his hand. His fingers ached and the palm of his hand felt the absence of the stick. How long had he been driving on manual? It was enough to drive a guy insane.

Roger took his own control stick. His own screen unfolded from the ceiling overhead. He took up just where Heinrick had left off—blinking the sleep out of his eyes.

As Heinrick ducked through the narrow corridor which lead to the ship cafeteria, he felt a tweak in the base of his back. On impulse, he grabbed for it with his hands, only stopping short of letting out a yelp of pain. As far as the service was concerned he was in tip-top shape and, although he trusted Roger—thought he was a good boy—he wanted to keep that particular ailment secret for as long as he could. If the service somehow found out he would be taken off the programme quicker than he could open his mouth to protest. He was over fifty now and well overdue for retirement. But he couldn't retire. Not yet. He lived for exploration, heading out on these half-crazed scouting missions into the deep recesses of space. He couldn't imagine himself on some colony eking out the rest of his days cultivating food with the rest of the old folks. He wanted to matter.

He got into the cafeteria—if it could be called that, considering that it consisted of nothing more than a dried food storage facility and a microwave. Once upon a time the coffee machine had worked, but it had been stripped for parts on some other desperate stage of a mission and no one had thought to repair it following the emergency. That had hurt on the first few days in the Albatross— as the smaller scouting ships were known—but he had got over the shivers and cold sweats eventually. He had never thought of himself as being addicted to anything, but those first hours had shown him up for the caffeine fiend that he was.

Heinrick dug out a packet of, what was supposedly, shepherd's pie. He eyed the design suspiciously: the yellow crust and thin coil of white steam rising. If it turned out anything like that then he promised himself that he would go take a spacewalk naked.

As he emptied the powder into the microwaveable container, he felt a buzz in his inner-ear—a transmission from command. He applied gentle pressure to his earlobe and said, "Captain Flaherty speaking."

There was a long stretch of static and then there was the synthesised voice. The computer back at command which was charged with giving navigational orders. "Albatross Fourteen-A, please check your maps and adjust course according to directional beacons."

Those 'directional beacons' were otherwise identified as the neon-green gridlines.

"Proceed along course until you are given further orders."

Heinrick removed his finger from his earlobe and returned to his sub-gourmet cooking. He was used to these various adjustments, how command had them jerking about all round the entire universe. Once, he recalled, they'd gone back over their tracks three times, and then a human operator had come onto the line and apologise, claiming that some sort of 'ghost' had got into the hardware. That happened infrequently, however. Whoever ran the computers knew what they were doing. For the most part anyway.

His dinner was ready in minutes, already inflated in its container. He tugged it out from the microwave tray—knowing from experience that it would be piping hot—and then he peeled back the lid and jabbed his fork into the mixture. It didn't look that bad at all—at least nowhere near the traffic accident which had been the nut roast last shift. Maybe he would have to partake in that naked spacewalk after all.

Roger called to him down the corridor.

At first Heinrick was a little irritated, considering that he'd spent the best part of the last day steering the damn ship, and he wasn't even to be given a moment's peace to get down some semblance of nutrition. He stuck a forkful in and then answered Roger with his mouth full. "What is it?" he said, his words muffled by his chewing.

"You'd better come take a look at this, captain."

"I'm eating!"

A long pause and then Roger said, "I'm sure your fat stores will suffice for the five seconds you need to see this, sir."

What a cheeky bugger, Heinrick thought. But, despite this mild outrage, he did deposit his fork into the foil tray and desert his shepherd's pie. He arrived back in the cockpit to observe Roger turned round in his seat, excitement sketched across his face.

Roger pointed to his screen. "Look, sir! Do you see that?"

Heinrick was somewhat weary. Roger had proven himself something of a trickster during their first few days on board together. Heinrick remembered the time when he'd been in the ship's toilet, depositing some solid waste, when he had noticed that the cleaning fluid had been used up. He had called and called out to Roger, from within the confines of the toilet, for him to top up the tank. In the end Heinrick had had to hoik up his trousers and go waddling off into the ship to do it himself. When he had returned to the cockpit Roger had grinned as he said, "You told me one of us always has to be at the controls, captain."

Heinrick leant over Roger's shoulder and examined the display. "Do I see what?"

"You can't make it out at that angle. Look through your own screen."

Now Heinrick saw what this was. A ruse to get him back at the controls, so that Roger might get on with whatever erotic fantasy had been playing out in his mind—no doubt with some foxy alien race that they were yet to discover. Nevertheless, Heinrick decided to indulge him. He didn't really think that there was much to be got out of jokes when there were only two of them.

He took up his seat and brought his visor down. The neon-green frames stretched out before him, making sense of the black-ness before them. And then, off to the side of his screen, he picked out a glimmer. He rotated the screen to take a closer look. As he brought the view round he saw that it was a star, off to the edge of his vision. How had he not managed to see it before? He guessed that he must've been so wrapped up into those green frames, keeping the stick level, that he'd had no time to take account of whatever might be round the ship. He had been focussed on his orders.

A lilting tone entered Roger's voice. "What should we do, captain?"

Heinrick remained transfixed by the star. It glowed a peachy-red. He had never seen such a tone of colour before, not even on their ultra-high definition film shows. It was the black backing of space which gave it its enormous strength.

"Sir?"

Heinrick peeled himself away from the image playing out before his eyes and glanced to Roger. "I think we should let command know about this."

Roger, clearly excited about this now, that they'd actually stumbled across something worth recording, fumbled through the communications board and brought up the line to command—the reserved line, the emergency line. This line was reserved because of the large amount of power it drained from the ship's battery. It got the transmission over to command more or less immediately but it couldn't be used for anything less than an urgent communi-cation. This qualified.

The synthesised voice on the other end answered a matter of seconds later. "Albatross Fourteen-A, what is your emergency?"

21

Heinrick leant forward and tried to calm himself, to speak clearly. It was important not to waste any more energy than was necessary. Every second they kept the line open drained their battery. "We've stumbled upon what we believe to be a dying star and would like to request a re-routing so that we might observe it for the sake of posterity."

There was a momentary pause and then the reply came. "Albatross Fourteen-A, you are to proceed on current course."

Heinrick waited, open-mouthed, for some further piece of information. But there was nothing forthcoming. There was only one thing which he could do now. He leant back into the communications panel and said, "Command, I'd like to request to speak with a human operator."

"Negative," the synthesised voice replied without hesitation.

Heinrick's palms sweated and the tweak in the base of his back tautened. There was only one explanation for the computer system blocking his request to a human operator and that was that the human operator had given a specific instruction to make it that way. Whoever was on the other end, back at command, wanted them to proceed along their computer-set course, no questions asked, no queries raised.

He clicked off the communication panel, knowing that to keep the line open any longer would only be wasting precious energy— they had their orders and they were expected to follow.

Roger stared at Heinrick, his eyeballs bulging in their sockets, waiting to be told what was coming up next, what they would do.

Heinrick resumed manual control of the ship, steering them over to the next green frame—they had drifted because Roger had got himself engrossed in the conversation with command. As they made up the ground, getting back on course, he shot Roget a sidelong glance. "What do you think?"

"About what, sir?"

"What should we do here?"

Roger considered the question, his eyes focussing on the dying sun in the visor. "I guess we've got our orders, and there'll be a hell of a lot of explaining to do if we divert from them."

"You mean *I'll* have to do a lot of explaining."

"Yeah," Roger said, scratching the back of his neck. "Don't you think command has got a good idea of what our job is, they can see the whole pie after all. Maybe they've got this dying sun covered, perhaps they've already sent another Albatross over there to check it out."

Heinrick couldn't help snorting a laugh. "Another Albatross in this precise section of space, a matter of light-seconds from us? Nah, that's impossible. Even command isn't that daft, they have at least a basic grasp on resource management—enough to know that sending a couple of Albatrosses to the same region of space at the same time is a tremendous waste."

"Then what?" Roger said.

"Well, I'm just speculating here, but I've got the feeling that whatever's happening with that dying sun they want us to stay well clear of it."

"Maybe it's dangerous."

"Maybe."

"So, it'd be better to follow our course, wouldn't it?"

"Probably," Heinrick said.

"Then why're we leaving the course, heading right for it?"

"Because we're curious, that's why."

2

A WARNING BELL rang out as they left their course. As Heinrick steered them into the haunting blue glow he had forgotten all about his half-eaten shepherd pie—his hunger—now all that was on his mind was exploration, to see what it was that command wanted to keep from them. He knew that heroes of exploration didn't become so without questioning orders once in a while—breaking ranks.

Roger sat in silence, just as captivated—Heinrick presumed—as he was.

The red light on the communication panel blinked on and off. It would be command wanting to know what was going on, why they'd left their assigned path. Heinrick knew that resources were stretched for command and they wouldn't risk sending out a fighter to intercept them, to come to their aid. And so all the power of reprimand command held was in their disciplinary chats, and they would only work if Heinrick let the communication through. Something which Heinrick had no intention of doing.

They drifted closer and closer, the green frames long forgotten. Now only a green arrow pointed Heinrick the direction back to their assigned course. He got a buzz knowing that he was going off the beaten track. Ideas of exploration and adventure flooded back to him—the very reasons he had signed up for service on the Albatrosses. He wanted to discover not just follow.

After a while the light on the command panel ceased blinking and Roger managed to snip the wire causing the warning bell to ring. They would have some explaining to do when they got back to Beta, but that could wait until then. Right now they had horizons to broaden.

It took them almost a whole day before they got close enough to properly make out their target, the star, through one of the windows. Now it was large, much larger Heinrick had imagined. There were tinges of blue creeping into it, round the edges and at the centre. He didn't need to crack open an encyclopaedia to know that this star didn't have long for the world. As they got closer, he dialled down their speed so they could take their time.

Once Heinrick had notified him that it was safe to take off his seatbelt, now that they had reached a lower cruising speed, Roger took off running through the ship, snatching up his camera—which hung up in his locker—as he went. Heinrick allowed himself a smile at he listened to the metallic *patter* of Roger's boots climbing the ladder up to the observation deck. Heinrick was sure—had he been in Roger's position, a couple of decades younger and more limber—he would've done the same. But here he was now, the captain, he had to retain his sense of perspective and stay on the bridge, at the controls, prepared for any eventuality.

The ship rolled as it thrust forward, closer to the star. Heinrick could feel the heat seeping through their thermal panelling and he repeated to himself—once again—that this was just what space exploration should be about, not mindlessly drifting through endless emptiness following green frames. He would have no trouble dealing with command, whatever their punishment turned out to be. This would all be worth it.

And then he heard a cry up on the observation deck.

A tingle ran up Heinrick's spine and he launched himself up out of his chair, all at once forgetting his responsibility as captain, the protocol to leave the cockpit manned at all times. He quickly regained his senses enough to check their current course—on manual—was sending them in a fairly straight direction. There seemed to be no debris on their navigational systems. He could leave things as they were for a bit.

His back blazing, he lugged himself up the ladder, feeling the breath leaving his lungs almost as soon as it entered. He hauled himself up over the lip and onto the observation deck, where the window gave a three-hundred-and-sixty-degree panorama of their surroundings. The star bore down on them from above, a mass of bright blue. Almost blinding.

Heinrick held up his hand to shield his eyes and looked to Roger who was pointing out through the reinforced window at some object. He was surprised that Roger could see enough to manage to pick out any details. Heinrick told himself that he would only be able to cope with this intensity of light for a few seconds more, then he would have to go back down to the cockpit.

"There!" Roger said. "Do you see it?"

Heinrick stalked up to the railing, feeling the piercing pain of the light burning at his irises. He squinted out through the window, in the general direction of where Roger pointed.

"A bit further over!"

Heinrick could see nothing for the light, and then, all of a sudden, he picked out the object. Something moving across the light, leaving its shadow behind. If it hadn't been moving he never would've spotted it. He managed to put the pain of the intense light to the back of his mind and to continue staring at the approaching object. It was a ship, wasn't it? It had to be. But, at the same time, it was impossible. It would've shown up on their navigational computers—the warning bell would've sounded to let them know there was another ship in the vicinity. And then it struck him, that Roger had disabled the warning system.

Roger was saying something but all that filled Heinrick's skull was action. He bounded across the observation deck and slid down the ladder back down into the cafeteria, his feet never touching the rungs, his grip all that kept him from sailing downward and cracking his skull against one of the surfaces.

He got back into the cockpit. The object appeared on their navigational screen now. He stared at the little green blob and he had no doubt that it was a ship. It was the speed it was moving, the nimbleness with which it made adjustments to its direction. And the fact that it was headed right for them. He noted, as he retook his seat and pulled down his visor, that the communications light was blinking away once more. He knew that command had just been trying to warn them, to give them advance notification of this obvious threat. His lungs reverberated as he called up to Roger—demanded that he get back down into the cockpit.

Roger was still grinning when he got back down, camera swinging from his neck.

Being the captain, Heinrick had to be the one to kill his buzz, to get their minds back onto the job at hand, and Roger did so—his smile vanishing from his lips as he absorbed the risk which Heinrick painted so clearly.

Heinrick jerked the control stick round, so that the ship turned its tail to the dying sun, and he switched power to the thrusters, sending them flying away from the incoming ship. His spinal cord felt like it might throb out through his flesh. He was determined to find a good chiropractor when he got back onto a colony—one which he could trust, and which wouldn't give away his secret to command, if command didn't decide to fire him for this breach of trust. Why hadn't he just thought to do as they'd said? Hadn't he realised that command had his best interests at heart?

Roger read out their distances as Heinrick guided them away. His voice still betrayed his excitement, and a faint tone of disappointment, as Heinrick himself was sure that he felt—at leaving this danger, so quickly slipping away at the first sign of trouble. But there was nothing else to do. Their protocol on being intercepted by third parties was to flee. They had no weapons on board, no substantial shields with which to protect themselves beyond light debris. They needed to run.

The communication panel continued to blink away incessantly.

Heinrick was on the point of snapping at Roger, telling him to find the wire and cut it so it would stop flashing.

Apparently sensing his thought process, realising that he had the communication panel on his mind, Roger said, "Captain, might it be the ship trying to communicate with us?"

"Might be," Heinrick said, scolding himself lightly at not having anticipated that eventuality—sometimes he got swept up in panic and rational thought took a back seat, never a good attribute in a captain.

"Should we open the channel?"

Heinrick looked over their navigational readings, at their position relative with the ship. He hadn't had a chance to look till now, previously being wrapped up in getting them away as quickly as possible. He saw that the ship had no chance of catching them up, that the Albatross was exponentially putting more and more distance between the two of them. Soon they would leave visual range, along with the dying star, and they would be back on course —albeit a little off their programmed track.

"Sir?"

"Okay, open the channel," Heinrick said.

Roger reached for the switch and tweaked it. He glanced to Heinrick, looking for a clue as to what was going to happen next.

In all Heinrick's years of being on the crew of Albatrosses, he could count his encounters with other ships on one hand. And those had never been unexpected—command had always given him advance notice of other ships in the area. This was his first contact with an unidentified craft, and it made him nervous. He was well out of his comfort zone. He thought that he'd refined that old saying of 'flying too close to the sun.'

Despite his shaking hands, he kept his voice steady and exact. "Unidentified craft, identify yourself."

They waited, neither of them daring to breathe.

Heinrick checked the monitors, ensuring that he kept up the same speed. It could be that the ship was feigning its losing of the race, trying to lull them into a false sense of security that the Albatross's capabilities were inferior to its own. He watched the energy meter. If this excursion had done anything, at least they had managed to recharge their batteries from the dying star—they would have enough for a lengthy emergency transmission, and more than enough to get back to command, if it were required.

Then, suddenly, through the nothingness came a burbling—all throaty sounds, inconceivable that they should be made by human facilities. Aliens.

Heinrick exchanged glances with Roger, who—without needing instruction—dialled up the translation extension, which immediately went to work identifying the language. It scanned for several minutes while the burbling continued. Not knowing whether what the aliens were saying might be threatening, he kept up the same speed. Now he really was on edge. It was one thing to be in contact with a human ship—one of the various factions, several of which were hostile—but to be in contact with an alien one was, well, an unknown quantity. Thus far humanity had taken the view that aliens were something to be avoided rather than investigated—at most studied from a distance, scanned for any form of threat.

The language extension cranked into action on the communications panel, letting them know with a bright *ping!* that the language had been successfully identified as Kintwit and the translation was in progress, catching up with whatever the captain of the ship on their heels was saying.

Hands sweating at the control stick, and eyes fixed on their route ahead, ready to punch the thrusters, channel all power to their engines if given the motive, Heinrick stretched his ears to hear the response.

"Help us," came the synthesised translation. "Please, help us."

3

HEINRICK'S HAND HOVERED over the thruster lever, ready to jab it forward, to set an emergency course right back for command. This was clearly a trick. Who in their right minds would ask for help from an Albatross? They had hardly space enough for two on board. But he hesitated.

"Help us," the alien captain said, once again.

Heinrick felt Roger's eyes on the side of his face, waiting for the executive decision, looking to his captain for their direction out of this situation. The sensible thing to do would be just to power right out, get back on course—maybe even dial up command right now, open an emergency line and inform them of the situation. Aliens would almost certainly get them a fighter out as quickly as possible. He stared at the communications panel.

"Help us."

"Sir?" Roger said.

Heinrick looked to him.

"Why don't we respond? Hear what they've got to say?"

Heinrick turned his attention back to the communications panel. "It's got to be a trap. Just . . . something about this situation feels all wrong. Everything's telling me to leave them far behind as fast as we possibly can."

"But what if they're in trouble?"

A memory from long ago leapt up and stung Heinrick. He recalled, when he'd been in the cadets, and he'd been out on one of his final training missions—in preparation for getting his stripes—he had managed to lose all control of his Albatross, the energy had merely drained from the system and he'd found himself floating out into space. He recalled the sensation, something like stepping into a sea and feeling himself sink and sink, knowing that, for all it mattered, the bottom was infinite. He had been out of control, forever slipping away from all he'd known. And then he remembered the steady sucking feeling as his ship had been drawn upward. He had looked about him, started to doubt his disbelief in any sort of god, thinking that some higher power had seen fit to take pity on him. Only when he had got himself together and managed to cobble together the bravery to leave his seat, to go check up on the observation deck, had he seen that it was a ship—an alien ship—that was saving him.

In that moment he thought of his anticipation, the wrenching feeling in gut that they might be saving him for some sinister purpose—indeed as humans did toward aliens, merely taking them into the labs to strip them of their languages, culture and biology, preparing for the war they were so sure would be coming—but they had brought him back to the waypoint, given him a gentle push and sent him on his way, back toward command. From then on, when he'd arrived back to command, his mission had been deemed a success and he had been accepted onto the next Albatross flying out. He had never told anyone of his brief encounter. It would've grated against everything that humanity believed of aliens. But Heinrick knew better or, at least, he thought he might.

Roger gazed at Heinrick with wide eyes. "Sir? I really believe we should speak to them. It couldn't hurt just to talk, could it?"

Heinrick broke from his daze. He managed the sliver of a smile. "No," he said. "I don't suppose it could." And then, with shaking hands, he clicked the communication panel onto transmit and spoke steady and clearly, so that the translation extension would manipulate his words into Kitwit. "This is Albatross Fourteen-A on lease from Beta Command Post. What is your emergency?"

The demands for help ceased and there was a long silence over the communication panel, and then there was the reply. "You are humans."

Heinrick wasn't sure—from the lack of intonation—whether the translation was faulty, if the statement had originally been intended as a question, or if it had merely been meant as a statement right from the outset. Either way he responded. "Yes, we are humans."

Another long pause, and then, "Have you come here, to finish us off?"

"What?"

"You have neglected to answer any of our distress signals. We sent out a beacon a long time ago and have heard nothing from Beta Command Post. We knew that humans were cold but we never expected them to be ruthless. On board we have the last remnants of our race, less than a dozen of us. Everything else was destroyed by the collapsing star. Our home world, everything. Now our ship is badly damaged. Maybe we have enough strength to go another light-year, but even if we can summon that power we shall have no more. We will merely drift about in space, to stave ourselves to death. So I must ask, are you pleased with what you have done, human?"

Heinrick's mind reeled at this account. Through everything though, all his shock at the callowness of his race, there was nothing that sounded remotely unbelievable. Indeed, it fit so nicely with their agenda—which was the survival of the human race itself, seeing any suffering of other races as an opportunity to put competition out of the picture. But Heinrick had always thought, even before those aliens had saved him from floating off into space, that space was so large, seemingly infinite, that surely there was room enough for everyone to be tolerated. If those aliens hadn't saved him back on his training mission then he would've drifted off into space, been left for dead—the same fate these aliens, these Kitwit, faced right now. He knew that there was only one thing he could do.

Sweat beading on his forehead, and rolling down his cheeks, he clenched the control stick tight and swooped the ship round, taking them in a one-hundred-and-eighty-degree turn, bringing them head on with the Kitwit ship.

Roger tensed beside him, he observed his hands gripping tight to the sides of his seat, and his features all gaping wide. This was all so far from Roger's training—going against everything he had been recently taught in the academy—that Heinrick had no wonder that he was reacting this way. Roger was a good kid because despite all his indoctrination, his heart had told him the right thing to do. It was more than Heinrick could say for himself, if Roger hadn't held him back, allowed himself a second thought, to scour his own memories, then he never would've thought to save these Kitwit from oblivion.

Heinrick kept his eye on the navigational screen, watching as he locked onto their ship, concentrating the ship's course onto the Kitwit. They got closer and closer, and soon he could make them out without the aid of the computer systems. Their ship—indeed—looked damaged, and the analysis confirmed it. They had damage to their thrusters, their life support systems, their—well, just about everything was damaged beyond repair. Now he knew that the Kitwit hadn't been exaggerating in saying that they would be dead soon. Roger and Heinrick were their only hope.

Heinrick felt the ship vibrate round him as he turned on the reverse thrusters. He brought them up alongside and then caught up with the Kitwit's speed. He had Roger press the appropriate buttons to send out the walkway. Without speaking, both he and Roger rushed up to the observation deck where they watched the snakelike tube slip out from the Albatross and toward the gate in the side of the Kitwit ship.

A slight jerk passed through the Albatross as it locked into Kitwit ship, and Heinrick watched on, his fingers wrapping round the railing, all his muscles tight—the pain in his back now reduced to a mere throb.

There was a long wait wherein no one stepped into the walkway, and Heinrick convinced himself several times that, in fact, this had all been a big mistake—that the Kitwit had succeeded in drawing them close only to attack them. He reminded himself of the damage to their ship, that they were on their knees. If the Kitwit decided to blow the Albatross up it would spell their own doom too. He gritted his teeth and forced himself to hold his nerve, not to rush back down to the cockpit, to break off the walkway and shoot back off toward Beta Command. He owed to the universe and now was his opportunity to pay the debt.

The walkway windows betrayed a series of shadows passing down it, coming toward the Albatross. Another prospect struck Heinrick, that they might be letting the Kitwit in only for them to commandeer the ship, to kill both him and Roger. He checked himself, told himself that now they were in the walkway there was nothing he could do. In any case, as representatives of the human race, wouldn't that be no more than they'd deserve? What had they shown other races of the universe? Didn't these Kitwit merit taking control of the Albatross, heading off into space at the expense of just another couple of human sadists?

The airlock remained shut tight. Both he and Roger turned their attention in its direction. The red light glowed and then, all of a sudden, switched to green. A voice over the speakers requested permission to come aboard. Heinrick exchanged glances with Roger and then acknowledged the request. The airlock swept back.

Seven figures stood there. They were perfectly black, seemingly unclothed. They stood on a single foot—if it could be called that. They seemed no more than translucent shadows, no discernible features. Their bodies were oblong shapes. From between them, Heinrick wasn't sure which specific Kitwit made a sound, a series of the familiar throaty sounds quivered through the air. He tapped his earlobe a couple of times and called up his translation extension. When he looked over at Roger, he saw that he did the same. And then he glanced back at the Kitwit, ready to hear what they had to say.

"Thank you for saving us. You are a credit to your race."

Heinrick's throat dried up. He looked between the Kitwit, trying to determine the leader, but—not being able to—he stared into their assembled mass and said, "It's a pleasure. An absolute pleasure."

The Kitwit floated onto the observation deck.

Heinrick looked round, feeling a little ashamed that he had nothing to offer them. This was a once-in-a-lifetime opportunity. Although the existence of alien races in the universe was a known fact among even the youngest children of the human race, almost no one had ever met an actual, live alien—their access kept restricted to scientists and warmongers. He supposed he had envisaged tiny green men, something resembling a human, nothing like these *gases* which confronted him. At least they would have no trouble in accommodating them on the Albatross.

He looked up, through the windows to the dying star above them, still giving off its blue light. Quivering rays licked at the edges of its form. He told the Kitwit to get comfortable and then, tugging Roger alongside him, made his way back down to the cockpit. He watched on the screen as the Kitwit ship swung away from them, back toward the dying star. Once more the communication panel was flashing, and he knew it was command, wanting to know what was going on. Heinrick simply dragged the control stick back round and sent them back off, onto their course again.

After they'd proceeded in silence for a stretch, Roger looked to him. "So, what now?"

"I guess we just carry on with the mission."

4

THEY DID JUST THAT, drifting on through space, going
through the same green frames on the navigational screens.
Heinrick had no idea where they were headed, and it was only
when they were about three quarters of the way back that he
realised they were going back toward Beta Command Post. He
looked to Roger to point out this fact.

Roger shrugged and said, "Not the first time command's sent
us out on a dead rubber, is it?"

Heinrick checked out the navigational screen. He checked
their energy levels. "Good thing too, I guess. We're running low on
pretty much everything. Don't want to think where we might've
been if we hadn't sucked up some energy from that dying star."

Later on, Beta Command Post appeared on the navigational
screen beside another object. Heinrick zoomed in. Another ship.
This time it was identified. He checked over its code and estab-
lished that it was a fighter. It wasn't out of the ordinary for
command to send out a fighter to guide them in. Those pilots got
so bored with nothing to do that they got sent out on the most
banal of assignments. He saw the communication panel blinking
away and he answered.

"This is Captain Flaherty of Albatross Fourteen-A," Heinrick
said.

The response was immediate, almost cutting off Heinrick's
own transmission. "Captain Flaherty? This is Fighter Nine-B. We
understand that you are carrying unauthorised cargo. Permit us an
approach-and-board for quarantine protocol."

'Quarantine protocol.' Heinrick knew all about that—just
where it led. It would involve several troops boarding the ship and
taking the Kitwit into custody. What would happen to them next

would be anyone's guess. He stalled for time, aware of Roger looking to him for instructions. Then he said, "Fighter Nine-B? I'd like assurances of the safety of our cargo. What's going to happen to them?"

"None of your concern Albatross Fourteen-A."

"Negative," Heinrick said, feeling a chill pass up his spine, "it is my concern. You see, I saved these Kitwit from destruction. If I had kept to the course programmed on our navigational systems, they would be dead by now. So I would like—"

"Albatross Fourteen-A, you have your orders. Authorise our approach and set your systems to receive our boarding party."

Heinrick gripped the control stick and eyed the navigational screen. He saw the fighter drawing closer by the second. Soon they would be upon them. He knew full well that they had the powers to override the Albatross's systems. If Heinrick resisted they would merely take the Kitwit from them, unless . . .

Heinrick glared at Roger. "Do you think you could isolate and sabotage the remote control system?" he said.

Roger's Adam's apple bobbed. "Sir?"

"Find the system and sabotage it. Then the fighter will have no option but to gain our cooperation. They won't be able to tell us what to do anymore. We'll have leverage."

"But sir, when we arrive we'll receive serve reprimand, we'll—"

"I'll receive the reprimand. You will just have been acting on my orders. I promise to make it clear to the tribunal that you had no role in any of this. The only career it'll affect is mine."

Roger seemed to understand this and he leapt up from his seat and dashed into the belly of the ship to get to work.

Now it was a race against time. Heinrick watched the fighter sneak closer. If they managed to get within range, override their systems before Roger had sabotaged the remote protocol then they would get boarded all the same—the Kitwit would end up in custody and he and Roger's careers within the Albatross programme would be at an end. He squeezed the control stick and hoped that Roger would get his work done quickly and efficiently.

The fighter was nearing their sphere of influence when Roger bounded back into the cockpit, red-faced and sweating all over. He was out of breath as he spoke. "I've . . . done . . . it . . . sir."

Heinrick could hardly restrain himself. He reached out and clapped Roger on the shoulder. "Brilliant!" he said. "Just brilliant!"

Roger collapsed into the chair beside him. "What do we do now?"

"We wait."

Sure enough the communications panel blinked again. With nothing to lose, Heinrick answered. "Albatross Fourteen-A here."

"Authorise our approach or we shall override your systems."

"We want our cargo to be granted resident status."

"Negative."

Heinrick sucked in his gut and then puffed out his cheeks. "Then you'll have to snatch them from us. We're not giving them up."

"Fine," the fighter responded.

Heinrick watched as the fighter levelled off with their speed, drew up alongside them. Nothing at all happened. He restrained the urge to reach across and ruffle Roger's hair—not wanting to get too carried away yet. Sure they had got the upper-hand, but that by no means mean that they'd got what they wanted.

The communications panel lit up again.

Heinrick stuck his finger in his ear.

"Albatross Fourteen-A, we're detecting an error with the remote control programme."

"Is that so?"

"We must remind you that any unauthorised interference with

any part of the ship shall be met with a tribunal back at command. Do you understand?"

They weren't totally thick, then. They realised that they weren't simply going to hand over the Kitwit. "I do," Heinrick said.

"Then you deny that there has been any sabotage to your systems."

"I'd say that's irrelevant."

A pause then, "Would you repeat that?"

"It's irrelevant."

"How so?"

"We are demanding safe passage for our cargo and until such a time will not authorise anyone on or off this ship."

The communications cut out. Heinrick knew that they were having a conversation with command, working out how they were to proceed. This wasn't something which happened everyday and, as such, needed to be treated with utmost delicacy. He watched the navigational screen, hoping that the fighter would peel off from them, lead them into command. But it kept up its same flight path, resilient to Heinrick's demands.

Another communication arrived.

"Yes?" Heinrick said, feeling that he had just cause to feel a touch smug.

"This is the final request," the fighter said. "You are to allow us on board."

"Negative."

"Last chance."

This was the endgame now. They would be forced to escort them back to command.

"Um, captain?" Roger said, pointing to the navigational screen.

The fighter had swooped round so that it faced up to the Albatross. For all intents and purposes it looked like an attacking approach. Heinrick knew what was going on now. They were going to blow them out of existence. Even he had underestimated humanity's paranoia. So be it. If they wished to destroy them that was what would happen. But at least, he, Heinrick Flaherty, had done all he could to promote peace and understanding throughout the universe. He closed his eyes and waited.

"Go on," Heinrick said. "Shoot us. We're ready."

COPPER WORLD

Harry's shadow leapt over lakes and swooped low over mountains, dusting its feet in snow. It descended and descended, almost colliding with hard rocks below, only to curve back upward at the very last moment. The whistle of air trailed in the shadow's wake.

1

A DRAUGHT DRIFTED in beneath the door, carrying with it the faint buzz of traffic. Harry's temples throbbed and his skull ached. He tugged his blanket up to his chin and turned onto his side.

The mobile phone whirred on the bedside table. A blue-white glimmer beamed through the brownish gloom.

Harry shielded his eyes and waited for it to ring itself out.

It rang again, and again.

He flung off the blanket and snatched the phone. "Wha?"

The person on the other end spoke just above a whisper. "Is this Harry Dunston?"

Harry swung his legs around and sat on the edge of the mattress, sending the springs squeaking as he went. "Yes, what do you want? Who is this?"

"Dunston. My name's Shields. From Pyko Tech."

He flinched. That name, *Pyko Tech*, resonated through his mind. It jabbed him over and over, never relenting. "Look, I'm off ill today. Can't this wait?"

"No, Harry," Shields said. "You're not ill."

"What're you talking about? Of course I'm ill. I've got a splitting bloody headache. Is this some kind of test? Are you checking that I'm not bunking off?"

"No—"

"Then what is it, for goodness' sake?"

Papers rustled on the other end of the line and Shields dropped his voice to a husky, grumble. "Harry, listen, there's not much time. Your life is at stake."

"What?"

There was a lengthy pause.

Harry glanced at the mobile screen. It was an unidentified number. He wondered if this were some kind of windup call. But he had no idea of anyone who would call him for a joke.

"Harry?"

Harry closed his eyes, attempting to banish his pounding headache. "Yes, I'm still here."

"You've no longer in our—my world."

"What?"

"I know this sounds ridiculous, Harry, but you've got to believe me. They found out about you going to the journalist, they instructed me to send you to the Copper World."

"The Copper World?"

"Yes, where you are now. You probably haven't noticed, but the whole place has a coppery tinge to it. Turn on the light, Harry."

Now convinced this was a windup, he reached out and flipped the light switch.

However, just as Shields claimed, the whole flat was awash in a coppery glow.

"What's going on?" Harry said, his grip tightening on the handset.

"Don't panic."

Harry reached up to his eyes and brushed his fingertips across them. "You've given me contact lenses, something like that, haven't you?"

"Harry, please, I know this is emotional—"

"What is this? What're you doing to me?"

"I'm sorry, I had no choice. Clawsley ordered me to send you there. You should never have spoken to the journalist."

Clawsley? His mistake couldn't have reached that far—gone

right to Pyko Tech's managing director. Harry thought back. Two weeks ago he had botched an experiment investigating human reanimation. His boss had gone ballistic, written him up, complained about the process from start to finish, questioned the cost and even Harry's credentials.

That had been the end of the road for Harry, he had had enough with the administration at Pyko Tech, their misunderstanding of science, and had sold the story—top secret research—to an eager journalist. Harry had been well-paid and had intended to leave Pyko as soon as he could, find a job somewhere else, maybe even leave the country.

"What have you done?" Harry said, his voice sticking in his throat.

"I used a transporter. Sent you to the Copper World."

"You keep talking about this Copper World as if it were something everyday, that I should instantly know what it is."

Shields muttered something to himself or, perhaps, to someone beside him, out of earshot. "I don't have much time, Harry."

"Then start talking."

Shields sighed. "Think of the Copper World as a shadow of our own. It's the next level down from our own reality. It was discovered around a hundred years ago, observed, and only now have I"—he hesitated—"*we* managed to find a way of sending beings to it."

"And that's what you've done to me?"

"Yes."

"Why?"

"Because of the journalist. You betrayed Pyko."

Harry scoffed. "So that's it? You banished me here, like leaving a mutineer on a tiny tropical island?"

"That is an apt comparison."

"And I'm going to starve here, then?"

"Not quite."

"Then what?"

More mumbling, another paused, and then, "The only means to send a being from the real world to the Copper World is to split their Copper World-self from their real-world self. We call the Copper World-self a 'shadow.'"

"Well, I'm the real-world self, correct?"

"Yes, Harry."

"Then what about my shadow?"

"It's on the other side of the world."

"And what does that mean?"

"It means that it's searching you out, drawn to you like a magnet."

A fresh wave of migraine struck Harry. He massaged his temples. "And?"

"When the two parts meet, within the Copper World, it will result in spontaneous combustion."

"I'll die?" Harry said.

"Worse. You shall disappear from existence."

Thoughts jetted around Harry's brain. He tried to make sense of what Shields told him, that he was being hunted by his own shadow. Just like deadlines always did, the strain of time pressure forced him into practicalities. "How long have I got?"

"About three days."

Harry gritted his teeth. "Is there any way out?"

"As yet the transporter is unidirectional."

"Right."

"I'm sorry, Harry."

Harry thought over his situation, trying to get everything straight. As he saw it his only way out was to find the transporter, somehow stick it into reverse and escape his situation. He got to his feet. Balancing the phone between his shoulder and ear, he shrugged on a pair of jeans and shoved his feet into his battered trainers.

Shields was still speaking, his voice seemingly getting quieter with each syllable. ". . . As a human being within the Copper World you can still physically affect your surroundings, affect the real world, though you will appear invisible to us."

"And why are you telling me all this?"

Shields sniffed. "It's wrong what we're doing. But I can't escape. I thought you had a right to know what was happening to you, to have some peace before you died."

"You wanted to lighten your conscience?"

Shields remained silent.

Harry tied his trainers tight. "I'm coming over to Pyko."

A note of alarm rose in Shields's voice. "No, Harry, please, there's nothing I can do for you. You'd get us both into trouble."

"But I'm invisible, right?"

"Well, yes, but—"

Harry hung up the call, pulled on a frayed jumper and headed out the door of his flat. Being a scientist himself he knew that Shields was holding out on him—scientists always knew just a little more than they cared to share and he was determined to seek it out. It was his life at stake after all.

As Harry emerged in the midday sunshine, he took in the true nature of his surroundings. Everything was as Shields had suggested—a heavy copper glow following all the figures around him. He headed into the park which ran alongside his block of flats. Bushy green-brown trees surrounded a sparkling brown pond. Glossy-maroon ducks quacked for bread. Copper children splashed in the shallows. Their forms held steady for the most part but every few seconds, like a television screen moving between sweeps of static, the copper shadows would becoming hazy, like clouds of steam, before reassuming their true form once more.

Harry squinted, trying to keep the image straight, but it was impossible, ever-changing. His brain felt warm and fuzzy. His eyeballs burnt into their sockets. He collapsed to the ground and blacked out.

The shadow's reflection glistened in the water. Its face was darkened, malformed, ever-changing. The shadow shifted in waves, through the air, darting from side to side, as if caught in a passing breeze, but always returning to its steady and true direction, always moving forward, drawing closer.

2

HARRY CAME TO and grasped his head in his hands. He looked about, sure that someone must have seen him go down, but everyone continued about their business—the brown forms moving back and forth, blurring one into the other, tangling and untangling.

Shaking, he found his feet and glanced around. He caught sight of the metro and headed for it, remembering that he had to get to Pyko Tech as quickly as possible—to get some real answers from Shields.

Getting into Pyko Tech was much easier being invisible. He simply skipped through the metal detectors, past the several security checkpoints and arrived in the main lobby—staffed by half a dozen receptionists and twice as many security guards. He headed off to the interactive maps, logged into his account using his fingerprints and called up Shields's entry on the directory. He read off his office location, checked his file photo: a balding man with flabby jowls and thick-framed, square glasses, and then made his way through the building to find him.

As always, the corridors were busy. Several times he brushed scientists or lab assistants. Whenever he made contact they would stare around themselves, frown lines would appear in their foreheads, then they would shake off the sensation and continue travelling wherever they were going.

Before long Harry located Shields, stooped over the back of a chair, with his hand resting on the shoulder of a younger blond man dressed in a lab coat, operating the computer.

Harry snuck up to Shields's side and brought his lips close to his ear. "Shields?"

Shields stiffened. "Wh—H—Harry?"

"That's right."

"I told you not to come."

"You also told me I was a condemned man."

The younger man craned his neck to observe them. He looked through Harry and then back at Shields. "Is he here?"

Shields nodded. "Yes, Jack."

Harry kept focussed on Shields. "I know you've got a theory on how to get me back, and I want you to try it."

"What makes you think—"

"Don't lie to me, Shields!"

Shields nodded to himself again, several times, cleared his throat and then said to Jack, "Hold the fort here, will you? This shouldn't take long."

They passed along another long series of narrow corridors, all teeming with scientists, bustling back and forth. Shields held his finger up to a scanner and they entered a seemingly anonymous room.

The room was empty save for a contraption in the very centre. It reminded Harry of an iron lung. He supposed this to be the transporter. "What do you have in mind?"

Shields rounded the transporter and then slid its transparent visor back. "I don't know, perhaps reversing the process will do it."

"Should I get in?"

"Yes," Shields said, busying himself with the control pad beside the machine.

Harry slipped onto the soft bed beneath the transparent visor. He lay back, resting his head against the pillow. His body juddered with tension. He tried to slow his breathing, to relax his heart rate, but it was impossible. If this didn't work he would be doomed.

A few minutes later, Shields snapped the visor into place, sealing Harry within. Only the distant click of computer keys and the odd cough from Shields broke the silence. The machine hummed to itself, getting louder and louder.

Harry shut his eyes and lost himself in the vibrations.

The shadow bobbed and swayed as it soared higher and higher, into the clouds, its form melding with the white-brown mist. It dived and ducked through the air, like a leaf caught in a gust, before being sent cruelly twirling back down to earth.

3

A TREMOR SHOOK HARRY. He wrenched his eyes open to see Shields rounding the machine and then flipping back the lid. The familiar brown sheen clouded everything. "It didn't work, did it?" Harry said.

Shields shook his head. "I'm sorry."

Harry had dreaded this moment. All hope evaporated. He felt numb, cold. "What now?"

Shields examined Harry and then sighed. "We could—"

Out of the speaker beside the sliding door to the lab a synthesised voice announced, "ACCESS DENIED."

Harry focussed on the door. "Who is it?"

"Don't know," Shields said, plodding his way across the lab and studying the access monitor. He waved for Harry to hide himself.

Harry thought about it, considering he was invisible it seemed unnecessary, but he supposed that whoever was about to walk in could well bump into him. So he took up his position in an alcove between two work benches.

Shields buzzed the door open.

Managing director of Pyko, Richard Clawsley, strutted in.

Harry had never seen him in person, but he recognised him from the in-company training videos.

Clawsley wore a dark blue, double-breasted suit with gold buttons. The shoulders of the suit were so rigid it seemed that Clawsley had forgotten to remove the coat hanger before putting it on. As he strolled through the lab, he held his right hand curled in the recess of his lower back. He approached the transporter and squinted at it. "Quite an incredible device, this."

"Yes, sir," Shields said, sauntering toward him. "A really remarkable feat of engineering."

Clawsley glowered at him.

Shields's Adam's apple bobbed. "I mean, a remarkable feat for Pyko Tech."

Clawsley laid his fingers on his pitted chin. "The reason I'm visiting is because I was informed that this laboratory reached high levels of electrical usage a matter of minutes ago." He stared at Shields. "I thought I would come and investigate personally."

Harry crunched his teeth. He had only spent a matter of moments in Clawsley's company but already he didn't like him. There was something slippery and untrustworthy about him.

Shields writhed his hands. "Sir, it was just a routine test—"

Clawsley held up his palm. "You were under strict instruction not to touch the device until advised."

"But, sir—"

Clawsley approached one of the side benches, where a document reader lay. "I believe the demonstration with Harry Dunston showed the capacity of the device quite satisfactorily." He rested his hand on the reader. "Plans all here, are they?"

"Yes."

"All documented to Pyko Tech's high standards?"

"Yes, sir."

Clawsley reached into his jacket and produced a blaster pistol. He pointed it at Shields. "Get in the machine."

Shields opened his mouth to complain.

"Quickly, I haven't got all day," Clawsley said. "You've proved yourself not to be trusted, all this sneaking around playing with things against orders."

Shields remained still.

"Come on," Clawsley said. "I would have thought after a lifetime sitting on your backside reading and theorising about this copper-place you might be anxious to get a proper look, first hand."

Eyes falling to the floor, Shields ventured over to the transporter, and then lay down.

Harry's muscles tautened. He had to do something. Sure Shields had been the one who had sent him here, to the Copper World, but he had just been following orders—like all the other researchers at Pyko. He slunk out from his hiding place and stalked over to the transporter, taking care to stay out of Clawsley's reach.

Clawsley yanked down the visor of the transporter then crooked the document reader in his arm and read off the instructions. He tapped away at the computer console. "I've been thinking about your strategy, your theorem surrounding this process. All this stuff about a shadow version hunting the real one then blowing it up is perfectly nice, but it seems a little sticky, too unsure. A touch slow. I was doing a lot of thinking about what you said, that as the victim awaits their shadow-self they may remain in contact with the physical world. In fact this might well be the perfect opportunity to experiment." He rounded the machine.

Harry ducked out of the way.

Clawsley dialled another series of commands on the computer pad.

The transporter hummed. Electricity crackled through its wires.

Although Harry knew he had to save Shields, prevent him from being condemned to the same fate, he hesitated, caught up in the spectacle of the machine.

A strange purple-orange glow emanated, hung in the air all around, and then, all at once, evaporated. The charge in the air disintegrated. When the mist cleared Shields remained in the same place.

Clawsley clicked off the safety on his blaster and slid back the shield. He aimed at where Shields lay and fired.

Blood rushed into Harry's cheeks and he dived forward, barging into Clawsley's back, knocking him flat.

Clawsley stumbled to his feet, blaster dangling from his fingers. He held the blaster up to his eye and looked along the barrel. "Shields? That you? You managed to get out of the transporter, I see. You sly little devil."

Harry looked beyond Clawsley, to Shields who still lay on the transporter. He had a large blaster wound in his left shoulder and he was gasping for air.

Clawsley fired into the air, at the other side of the room to Harry.

The blaster shot burnt into a side bench and sizzled.

Harry stayed still.

A faint smile crept across Clawsley's lips. "You're doomed Shields, whatever happens now." He glanced back at the transporter. "I think I'll revise the design, somewhat, add some buckles to keep the subject held down. How does that sound?"

Lying on the transporter, Shields spluttered.

Clawsley pivoted, still holding the gun firmly. "Looks like I did get you after all." He stepped closer to the transporter and bent over Shields, ear cocked. "It sounds like I caught you pretty smartly."

Shields gargled something.

"What was that?" Clawsley said, pocketing the blaster.

Again Shields said something out of Harry's earshot.

Clawsley cackled. "Oh, don't you worry about the research, it's all in safe hands. I hear your boy, Jack, is quite a scientist. Perhaps he's ready to step into his father's shoes, eh?"

This time Shields had no strength to vocalise. His whole body shuddered.

Clawsley exited the lab.

As the door slid shut, Harry bounded over to Shields and crouched down beside him. Tears prickled at the corners of Harry's eyes and his hands shook.

Shields turned his head to look at him. He managed a weak grin. "Looks like I got to see this place, after all."

"Is there anything I can do?"

"No."

Harry rested his hand on Shields's. "Clawsley says you have a son."

"Jack . . . you saw him . . . in the lab."

"Can he help me?"

Shields's lips moved but no sound formulated. There was an elongated croak and then Shields's muscle relaxed and he exhaled his final breath.

Harry lingered a few moments and then withdrew his hand. He headed up to the door and tried the security monitor. It required a fingerprint. Harry had no access to this lab. He looked for some emergency switch but, finding none, he returned to the transporter.

He shovelled his hands beneath Shields's armpits and hoisted his sizeable frame upward, off the transport. He dragged Shields's body across the room, propped his hand up onto the scanner and pressed his finger to the device.

The door hissed open.

Harry considered what to do next. Every nerve in his body told him to run. But he couldn't. He had to leave Shields where Clawsley had last seen him. So he lugged Shields back onto the transporter and then crossed his arms over his chest. He wondered whether he should do something more. Finally, he reached over and rolled Shields's eyelids shut.

When Harry got back out to the labs he searched for the blond boy, but could find him nowhere. He found an unattended computer station, out of sight from the rest of the lab, and did a search on the directory. He saw that Jack was not in the office—he had been sent home.

For privacy reasons the system held no details of employees residencies, so he headed back to the reception area and stole his way in behind one of the receptionists. He waited there for what seemed like hours, waiting for one of them to get up and go on a break. When she did, he snuck in and got the information he needed. As he rose, one of the receptionist's turned her head, looked right at him, surely having heard him tapping away on the computer. But he was gone before she had a chance to investigate further.

Harry arrived outside Jack's house and worked his way through the side gate to a door round back. Just as he reached out to knock, he lost his balance and fell away once more.

The shadow dipped down the hill, slowing its pace. Its form wobbled about its frame, never settling in a single position. The shadow got closer to the ground, so that it was almost walking, its shadow feet touching the grass below. And then it snapped its neck upward and rose again.

4

HARRY BLINKED AWAY his daze, knowing that the shadow got closer every second. He rapped a couple of times on the door and waited.

Jack opened the door and looked out, his forehead wrinkled. He stuck his neck out and looked left and right. From this profile Harry saw the tear tracks worming their way down either cheek. He had lost his father today and Harry was sure that Clawsley had been the one to tell him—sent him home as a kind gesture. Should Harry just walk away? Leave this poor kid to get on with his life?

"It's me," Harry said.

Jack jumped. "What? Who's there?" And then his eyes narrowed. "Dunston?"

"Yes, it's me."

"Wha—what happened to my father?"

"Hasn't Clawsley told you?"

"He said there was an accident."

Harry ran his tongue round his mouth. "Clawsley murdered your father."

Jack's expression remained neutral, his eyes far off, tears clinging to his cheeks. "How?"

Harry ran through the whole situation, how Shields had wanted to help him and how Clawsley had shot him after he'd transferred him to the Copper World. He had assumed that Jack might take some convincing, but Jack appeared to take it all on board at once.

Jack straightened, wiped the tears from his face. "Clawsley has made me head of the team. Put me in my father's place."

"Okay."

"He gave me the rest of the day off, you know, to think about things. He said he was sorry about my father but he has an important client coming in tomorrow and he needs me there, to lead the demonstration."

Harry wondered what that might entail—maybe shooting some hapless lab assistant into the Copper World. He turned his mind back to his own problems. "And do you have any idea on how to reverse the effects?"

A smile flickered at the corner of Jack's mouth. "I've been thinking of something, yeah."

"It's not just reversing the process, is it?"

"No."

Harry exhaled. "That's good to hear."

Jack invited Harry inside and he set him up in the guest room, promising to take him to work with him the following day. As Harry slept he was haunted by yet more images of his shadow getting closer and closer to him, its legs blurring with constant motion.

The next morning he travelled to work with Jack. They completed the normal routine, Jack writing up and sending feedback on his research from the previous day, before Clawsley arrived at Jack's desk, with a man with a buzz-cut, the client, walking beside him with his hands stuffed into his jacket pockets.

Jack's eye twitched as he bowed to Clawsley.

Harry had the urge to reach out and throttle Clawsley. But he held back, knowing that if he killed Clawsley, security teams would arrive, he would be found out. Pyko would be shut down and the machine would be put out of his reach.

With the client beside him, Clawsley ordered Jack to follow, like a dog behind its master.

Harry skirted them, passing through the same corridors to the room which held the transporter.

Once inside, Clawsley gave the client a forced smile. "Well, here it is."

The client approached the transporter, ran his hand over the visor, leaving a sweaty smear. "And it's fully-operational?"

"Oh yes," Clawsley said.

"Excellent."

Clawsley waved to Jack.

Jack skittered round the machine and approached the control pad then jabbed in a few commands. He stood back, his eyes wandering over the two men.

Harry kept as still as possible, hardly daring to breathe, knowing that a single sound might give him away, that Clawsley surely kept the same blaster tucked away in his pocket, ready to yank out at a moment's notice.

The client watched Jack as he worked. "The price remains as agreed?"

Clawsley's lips parted. "Ah, I'm afraid we've had to double it. Will that be a problem?"

The client glared at Clawsley, his eyes shifting about his face. "Will there be any further increases?"

Clawsley smiled, his crooked teeth jutting up from his gums. He placed his hand over his heart. "I can assure you that this will be the final price."

Harry had to admit that Clawsley knew how to turn the screw as a businessman, no wonder he had got so many intelligent people working under him. He chewed his lower lip and concentrated on staying still.

The client let out a satisfied sigh. "Good. But this had better work. I cannot tell you how many dead ends we have been along looking for a device such as this."

Clawsley patted the man on the shoulder. "You can tell your

president to rest easy. He has nothing to worry about. This machine is state-of-the-art."

The client flinched at the mention of his president and glanced over at Jack. "This will be kept confidential, will it not?"

Clawsley met his gaze, and the two of them stared at Jack. "Yes, Shields is most reliable. One of our most loyal. In fact his family have worked with me for three generations. Isn't that so, Jack?"

Jack cocked his head away from the control pad and blinked a few times. "I'm sorry, sir?"

"I was just confirming that client confidentiality is something we value highly at Pyko."

"Oh yes, sir."

Clawsley returned his attention to the client. "You see? Nothing to worry about." He rested his arm around the client's shoulder and led him toward the door of the lab. "May I interest you in any of our other products. Has your president considered a clone for instance? I must say . . ."

They left the room, and the door slid shut with a muted *beep*.

Jack backed away from the transporter. Sweat sparkled on his forehead and his eyes were webbed with blood vessels. "I've set up the program. Get underneath."

Although Harry had reeled through the story of Shields Senior's demise, he wondered whether Jack realised how much danger he was putting himself through here—that he might well find himself in the same situation, facing the same fate. Harry hesitated.

"Please," Jack said, his voice wobbling. "Just get on. If I can save you I'll be at peace with myself."

Harry did as he asked and the visor clicked shut.

The machine chortled into life.

The shadow approached a cityscape. Dark brown rays radiated off the windows of skyscrapers. The shadow slowed its pace. Its ghostly feet touched the ground, landing on a hillside. It walked, mimicking the human it represented, while its limbs failed to bend the long grass.

5

HARRY CAME AROUND to an alarm. It shook his skull, sending his brain slopping from side to side. For a second he was sure that he was back in his body, back in the real world. But the same brown film covered everything. He reached up and yanked the visor away, then glanced round.

Jack stood over at the door, stabbing at the keypad. He looked over to Harry. "Security team. They've found us out. They cut the transporter's power."

There was a shout from the other side of the door. "Remove the lock or we shall enter with force!"

Jack cowered.

This was Harry's opportunity to help out, to save Jack's life. Harry ran over to Jack and stooped over the door security panel. He turned to him. "Try to find a way out, I'll see if I can hold them off."

Jack nodded and ran over to the other side of the lab. But instead of leaping up onto the counter, trying to jimmy one of the air ducts open, he busied himself, tapping away at the transporter console.

"Go!" Harry said, frantically keeping up with the security team's attempts to override the security monitor.

"I can get the power back online!" Jack said.

"Don't worry about it. Get out!"

But Jack stayed where he was, typing away at the transporter.

Harry ducked down and concentrated on evading the attacks on the security panel—they had a hacker working to free the lock. He was afraid to turn around, that he might catch sight of Jack again, still playing with the damn machine.

A thick *hum* vibrated the air.

On the other side of the door, Harry heard a voice, perhaps the hacker, "They've got the power back online, you're going to have to bust it down."

The door buckled.

"Now!" Harry said, turning to Jack.

Jack said, "I'll leave the document reader on the side, with the instructions on how to reverse the process, if you can find your way . . ."

There was a *boom* and the door rocked on its hinges. Another hard impact in its centre and it gave way, crowning into the lab. A member of the security team barged inside. He wore a mask and carried a blaster rifle. He ran right into Harry.

Harry knocked his head against the counter and collapsed to the ground.

"Over here!" the security team member said. "Lying on the floor. I felt the impact."

Brown splodges flashed in Harry's vision. He tried to shake the sensation but it stayed with him. Darkness blotted the edges of his sight and he knew he was losing consciousness. Steady hands seized him and lugged him to his feet. As they led him away, out of the lab, he tried to catch a glimpse of the room, but couldn't move in the guards' tight hold. The chimes of tinnitus overwhelmed him.

The shadow entered the city, mingling with its people, losing itself in the crowds. It kept a steady pace, remaining focussed on its target. Whenever someone stepped in its path, it side stepped, like any polite city-dweller, before continuing unabated—becoming more at one with its human form with each step.

6

PYKO.
    Pyko Tech.
The label on the cupboard opposite stared at Harry as he lay in bed, bandaged up. There were more labels, all around the room, stamped onto various surfaces. His vision blurred and then came into sharp focus. He felt his wits return to him.

The door slid open and Clawsley appeared. Loose skin hung off his neck, reminding Harry of a komodo dragon. He swaggered over to the bedside and scowled down at Harry. "Enjoying the Copper World, Dunston?"

Harry's brain kept sloshing about, refusing to keep still.

"You might be invisible, but don't think you can simply disappear by being silent." Clawsley inspected his manicured fingernails. "I have been thinking about your career with us. It was such a shame you had to leave under such, uh, undesirable circumstances."

Harry eyed a pair of scissors on the bedside table. If only he could summon the strength to reach for them, he would have a weapon. He tried to move his arm, but it quivered and refused to obey him. He had hit his head pretty hard.

"But I believe in forgiveness and all that," Clawsley continued. "You're expertise is greatly valued, if your moral compass is somewhat wonky. I'd be prepared to give you another chance, return your old team to you, start you off on human reanimation again— comprehensively monitored, of course. What do you say?"

Harry's throat dried up. "And how would I do that. I'll be dead in a matter of hours."

Clawsley chuckled. "That's just the thing. You see, it seems that Shields Junior, before he left us, was kind enough to leave a document detailing the reversal process. So, really, Dunston, it's up to you."

Harry thought it over. Although he feared dying he was more afraid of being harnessed to Pyko Tech forever more, after what Clawsley had done to Shields. Whatever Clawsley had up his sleeve, there was sure to be a back up. The more he pondered, the more it became apparent that the only solution, the only way to set things straight once and for all, was to kill Clawsley.

He focussed all his strength into his left arm and reached for the scissors. He seized them in his grasp and stabbed Clawsley in the neck.

Blood welled up in the wound and ran down Clawsley's white shirt. Clawsley reached up to stop the flow, eyes bulging and gasping for air. He dropped to his knees.

Harry slipped off the bed and dashed for the door, leaving Clawsley to his fate. As Harry emerged into the corridor, his legs wobbled beneath him, he lost his balance and collapsed onto the smooth tiles.

The air around the shadow shimmered brown. It gave off waves, invisible to the passers-by. The shadow sleuthed out of shadow and into sunlight. Up ahead it viewed the enormous building, the placard declaring: *Pyko Tech*. Inside, it could sense its human form, calling out to it, tugging it closer.

7

HARRY RUBBED his eyes clear of the delusions. He had no time. If he could just get down to the transporter, he still held a hope. Everything was there for him. He leapt to his feet and dashed down the corridors, sending researchers flying and their document readers clattering to the floor.

His whole brain throbbed by the time he reached the lab. The door remained open, no one had fixed it since the security team had stormed inside. He slunk into the lab and ran up to the machine. He found Jack's instructions and punched them into the controls. The transporter lurched into life and Harry pulled himself underneath the visor.

The shadow passed through the reception, wound through corridors and approached the broken door to the lab containing the transporter. It hesitated a second and then crossed the threshold. Its human component lay still in the electric coffin. The air flashed and the human remained still. The shadow crept closer then reached out and merged.

8

HARRY FELT his arms and legs, and then stared around. Everything was back to normal, the world had returned to its regular shade. He rolled back the transporter's visor.

Footsteps sounded in the corridor. Clawsley rounded the corner clutching a blaster rifle.

All the air left Harry's lungs.

"Seen a ghost?" Clawsley said.

"Wha—how?"

Clawsley cocked the rifle. "A clone. I wanted to test your loyalty." He stared along the sight. "You failed."

Harry's heart thumped in his ears. There was nothing he could do, not up against a gun. He had only seconds to live. One or two breaths.

Clawsley's jacket flapped back and his blaster handgun floated from its holster.

Clawsley looked away from his rifle and gawked at the handgun. He had no time to turn the rifle before the handgun fired a shot into his stomach, and then another into his chest. The rifle slipped from Clawsley's clutches and he slumped to the floor.

Harry stared at the handgun, expecting it to turn on him. But it remained steady, still pointing at Clawsley's dead body. Then Harry's rational thought process caught up with him. "Jack?"

The handgun turned on the transporter, fired into its control panel. It fired again and again until it was reduced to melting metal and sparking wires. Then it blew apart the document reader.

The next few seconds seemed to unravel in slow motion. The handgun turned a hundred and eighty degrees, fired a last time, then clanged to the floor.

Harry's cry dissolved in his throat. He stooped forward, reached out and touched the emptiness. He felt Jack there, his hand. He leant in close and said, "Thank you," before snatching up Clawsley's blaster rifle and sprinting out into the corridor.

LITTERS

THE WHITE DRESS fit her well. Robin was at least sure of that much. As she stood looking herself over in the full-length mirror—her *mother's* mirror—she couldn't help but think of all those pictures she'd seen of her parents' wedding; of her mother's wedding dress in those pictures.

In a way, she could see the shadow of her mother clinging to her as she stood up here, breathing in the lilac perfume she had wafted over herself. Although they'd had a very 'special' breakfast, all she could really taste in her mouth was the wholemeal toast that they ate every day.

It was the little things.

The everyday things.

Those might all be gone before sunset today.

A slight draught got in under her dress and she felt it skitter across the surface of her skin, bringing her out in goose pimples. She gave a slight shudder and then tuned herself back into the sounds of the rest of the house—to where she could hear her three brothers all jabbering away among themselves. Boys could be so stupid. Even today, the day which might well be—was *seventy-five-per-cent* likely to be—their last day on Earth.

Only one of them would remain.

And, for some reason, she had already decided that it wouldn't be her.

That fate hadn't chosen her to keep on living.

So she must die.

Twenty-five per cent.

What was that?

It was nothing.

She gave herself a final lookover in the mirror and then, with a heavier heart than she had supposed, she left the room to join the rest of her family.

———

Just as she had imagined it in her mind's eye, the kitchen was a madhouse. Her three brothers—all of them white-tied and dressed in suits—wrestled one another in a pile on the floor.

Robin neatly stepped over their flailing limbs, not wanting to find herself dragged into the melee. On her last day on Earth, she wanted to go out with a reasonably clean dress.

Her mother, stood at a mirror sitting on the kitchen counter, prodding at her red lipstick with a piece of tissue paper, smudging it here and there. Her lipstick matched her flaming red hair: the same red hair which Robin had . . . and would be parted from later on in the day.

Forever.

Robin's father had his sleeves rolled to his elbows and he was finishing washing up a plate from breakfast. He stared out through the window, to the sprawling garden, losing himself in the greens all set in the golden morning sunlight.

Robin liked to try and get into other people's minds—liked to try and divine what they might be thinking at that moment in time. What else could he be thinking about other than which of them would be the one to survive?

Today they all celebrated their fifteenth birthday.

Their coming of age.

And for three of the four of them, their day of death.

Did her father feel any sadness at all about that? Surely he did.

In the books which Robin had read about people in the past, she had come to the conclusion that there had *always* been favourite children among parents. The reality that they lived merely echoed the fact of the matter: that love could not be evenly spread among all.

One always received more than the others.

When Robin looked to her brothers—her *pile* of brothers—she saw the one who was the most revered of them all: Eric.

He was the smallest and though his features were near identical to his brothers', there was something to his eyes, a certain *lightness* to them. His hair stuck up in tufts and could not be easily tamed by either a comb or a generous smothering of wax. And the other two brothers—Telmer and Henderson—could only have seen what Robin did.

It was so obvious.

Even now, she saw her mother glancing up to check on her dear Eric . . . concerned about whether something might happen to him.

With a percussive, and final-sounding *thud*, her father placed the final porcelain plate down in the drying rack, wiped his hands on a tea towel and then looked them over with—what Robin could only describe as—a *sad* expression.

"Time to go," he said.

———

Though Robin had passed by the Selection Centre every day for the whole of her life, on her way to school, she had never dwindled there long. For one thing, a pair of armed guards who wore bullet-proof vests, and carried large rifles, stood at the large gate. They wore sunglasses in a way which Robin found intimidating. She couldn't cope with not seeing people's eyes.

It *dehumanised* them.

As her father drove the car, the guards gestured for him to roll down the windows. He scrabbled about for his ID—couldn't find it momentarily.

When Robin glanced out through the windscreen, she eyed the white-washed building beyond—the concrete construction with its entrance, the door nestled further within partially obscured by shadow.

An ugly building.

But what else would it be?

What else had she *expected* it to be?

This was the place where she knew her classmates had wandered in, and then never returned.

Only the one *chosen* sibling emerging.

Though it was forbidden for them to speak about the matter at school, they had all heard the rumours. It was Georgia who had been the frankest with Robin after she had gone through the process herself.

Robin could remember that it had been after a PE lesson. She could still feel the light perspiration sticking to her skin, and smell the saltiness of her sweat. Her mouth tasted of manufactured raspberry from the gum which Georgia had passed to her just as they'd been leaving the changing rooms. The buzz of chatter filled the air as kids filed from one class to the next. And Robin couldn't help but smile up into the blue sky which stretched above—at the glowing sunlight which warmed her. But Georgia would take away all those smiles. Bring her back down to Earth.

Georgia had been to the Selection Centre about a week before, and, just like all the kids who'd been to the Selection Centre, she got somewhat evasive about school—never wanting to stick around to chat. It was understood, though, among the student body.

After all, who wanted to speak about the murder of their siblings?

Robin could only find herself agreeing when she heard talk of other kids saying that losing a sibling was like losing a part of themselves. What would happen, with the ones who would return to school, those who had been through the Selection Process, was that they would be reintegrated with the general student body, as if nothing at all had happened. Their siblings would be forgotten. All trace of them wiped from the records. How it happened, Robin had no idea—which was to say that she wasn't familiar with the process, only with its effects.

Kids disappeared.

They were simply *gone*.

But, when a kid came back from the Selection Process—the last one standing—they would generally follow the same patterns: want to be alone, appear despondent, and then, to somebody, somewhere around school—it might be a teacher or a student— they would open up, want to speak about the experience. If they went to a teacher first then the experience would be lost. The only way that knowledge got passed on was if that particular kid, that kid who had lost their siblings—their *identical replicas*—decided to speak with a fellow student.

And, that day, as things turned out, Georgia, for some inexplicable reason, chose Robin as the one for her to confide in . . . to tell her just what had gone on.

———

Robin's father's car was fairly new—at least it still carried that new-car fragrance. The seats still had a bit of an uncomfortable *scratch* to them, which she could feel through the frail material of her dress. She wanted—more than anything—to have some gum to chew on now. Just something to do with her mouth. But, since she had nothing at all, she decided to chew on her tongue, that faintly bloody, but intensely flavourless, taste.

The security men waved the car in through the gates.

Robin thought that she caught one of the men's eyes, even through his sunglasses. Nothing more than the whites of his eyes. But something . . . more than she had ever seen from one of those security men before.

The car purred its way over between the painted white lines, and her father switched off the engine and unbuckled his seatbelt. She wondered if her father had been through this day mentally many times before. If he had thought through just how things would turn out. She knew that, if she'd been in his place, she would've done the same . . .

He let them all out of the back seat, and Robin noted how a silence now lay over her brothers, as if—at last—they understood just what was going to become of them.

Perhaps they needed to be brought this close to death to experience some degree of gravity—the same gravity which had clung to Robin ever since that day Georgia had confided in her.

———

Georgia had tugged on her arm. Though she had worn a kind of frail smile, Robin had seen through it. She had seen how that smile had been concealing pain. The pain of loss. Like something had been physically cut from Georgia's flesh.

Indeed, as they'd slipped into the shadows which strung their way between the alleyway of a pair of buildings, Georgia's smile had soon faded away . . . really just *slipped* from her lips . . . and the tears had glistened in her eyes. Georgia had become skittish, looking out through the end of the alley, apparently in no doubt that they were on the point of discovery.

In the distance, there was the *clang* of the bell announcing it was time to commence the next block of lessons. But she couldn't have moved—even if she'd wanted to—such was Georgia's vicelike grip.

"I want to talk about it," Georgia said, "it seems important that I talk about it."

Robin had felt her chest tighten. Of course she knew the consequences, and that, really, there was little point of delving deeper into the details. Because she couldn't change anything. She couldn't change what was going to happen to her and her brothers.

Could she?

Robin half-heartedly attempted to guard herself. "Shouldn't you go and speak with a teacher—ask to see a counsellor if you want to discuss this?"

Georgia shook her head, sending her hastily arranged, blond pigtails dancing between her shoulder blades. "No. I wanted to speak to somebody—to *another kid*—a person who will pass through the process."

Robin could hear the sounds of kids' chatter fading now. She knew that in about a minute the whole school would be impossibly silent as the kids all went about their lessons—obediently following their teachers' instructions.

"Okay," Robin said.

———

The building was much bigger as Robin approached.

Somehow the doorway became thicker with shadow—more ominous the closer she got.

As she walked along the tarmac, toward the door, she couldn't help thinking to herself that she was doing this all of her own will —that her parents, that the two men standing on the gate—weren't about to shoot them if they attempted an escape.

Did that make her feel better?

Or *worse?*

Because, if there was something she could do to escape her fate —to help her *brothers* escape their fate—then why shouldn't she do it?

What would she have to lose?

She glanced over her shoulder, to the guards at the gate.

She wanted to . . . she really did . . . and yet, at the same time, she felt like her ankles had been weighed down by some invisible force—made to step forward: *one-two, one-two, one-two* . . . there was no other way.

————

In the alleyway between the two buildings, the air was fresh. It seemed to breathe life into Robin's skin. Though, like all the girls, she complained bitterly about having to do sport, she secretly savoured it. Not for the actual practice of sport itself—but for the time afterward. For how she felt afterward. Something approaching rejuvenation. Almost like—and she couldn't help the trite comparison—*rebirth.*

Georgia was reeling through the day—blow-by-blow—almost not having time to pause for breath. Somehow Robin found herself drowning in the details. She only picked out one particular phrase of Georgia's:

". . . You'll know the favourite," Georgia said, "I mean, that's what everybody told me—what all my brothers and sisters told me —they always said that I was my parents' favourite, but you can't really tell—*Can you?*—till it actually comes down to it, till they have to actually *choose* which one they want to keep . . ."

Again Robin found herself tuning out of Georgia's words, and yet, at the same time, she took in those extraneous details: the ones about how Georgia had had it explained to her, after she had been selected—and her siblings terminated—that this was the fairest way of solving global population. That every woman would have the right to a child. A child that the mother would be able to choose from among a series of copies—they had spoken to her about modified DNA; how they'd entered a new age of 'Survival of the Fittest'. It was all designed so that the mother might have the perfect child. *A child to cherish.*

Georgia had been told that she too would get the same choice, that—one day, if she wished to have children—she would be born with either triplets or quadruplets and—on their fifteenth birthday —she would face the choice of which she wanted to keep.

———

"Robin?"

Robin looked back, saw that her mother was speaking to her, urging her forward.

She hadn't quite realised that she had stopped in her tracks.

That she stood still right in front of the Selection Centre.

The two guards were staring at her.

She wanted to run—that was all she had on her mind.

And yet, at the same time, she knew it would be futile.

She looked over her parents' faces. She felt a slight tug at the base of her heart. She wondered if she really had been right all along—if she really had been right about them already considering Eric to be the favourite. Might they choose her after all?

. . . But Georgia had told her that she would *know*—for certain —who her parents' favourite would be. There really was no doubt. Not only she knew it, her brothers knew it too.

Eric was the chosen one.

And since Robin knew it to be true, would it be so wrong for her simply to make a run for it? To race toward the gate and the guards waiting there. Would being gunned down be a worse death than whatever they had in mind for her in the Selection Centre?

She turned to look at her family.

Her brothers were staring at her: Telmer, Henderson . . .

Eric.

They wanted to see if she would do it—if she was going to freak out.

Right now, she felt the strangest thing, this odd pull at her gut as if there was some deeply engrained survival mechanism working on her insides, trying to get through to her that she could be the one to live among all of her siblings.

Though she knew that was an impossibility.

She breathed in deep, saw the guards gripping tight to their rifles, and then she shut her eyes. It happened as one, in her mind, the gunshots rattled about her ears.

———

The next day, she returned to school.

She breathed in the cool air of the hallways, the endless rows of dusty, steel lockers. She kept a smudge of mint flavoured gum stashed in her cheek with the tip of her tongue. Everything was quiet, but that was because lessons had already begun.

It was strange to be back—to be one of the *chosen.*

One of those which her mother and father had chosen among her siblings.

Had it mattered that she had been the second choice? That Eric—*the supposed favourite*—had jigged away from them? With his parents cries in his ears, he had rushed the fence, attempted to clamber his way up . . . only to be shot down, to land on a crumpled heap on the floor.

Dead.

A pair of counsellors had emerged from the Selection Centre to see to Robin's out-of-control parents. They had been led inside. Made to go through the process just like everybody else.

As if Eric hadn't run from them . . . as if Eric hadn't been killed.

As they'd gone through the process, Robin's thoughts hadn't circled around just what was about to happen to her—that her death might be imminent—but on just what Eric had been thinking.

She wondered if he'd *known* . . . if he'd *known* he was the favourite.

Had he experienced the same doubts as she and her brothers had over just who was the favourite—however obvious it might be to see?

Or had he known all along.

Known that he *was* the favourite.

And been unable to take it any longer.

Couldn't face the pressure it might entail.

Of keeping four souls within his own—making up for the slaughter of his three siblings?

Whatever he had been thinking, the fact remained, Eric was dead now, just as Telmer and Henderson were. Only Robin survived.

Robin could hear the gentle *slap* of her hard-soled school shoes against the hallways. Her eyes twitched from side to side, scoping the terrain, searching for movement. There would be *somebody* around here, she was sure of it.

Somebody who might relieve her of her secret.

Of what had gone on the day before.

As she reached the end of the hallway and peered out—across the lush green lawn which occupied the area between the maths and chemistry blocks—she saw him.

A perfect target.

Unsuspecting.

Scuffing his feet along the path as he walked.

She couldn't help but feel a slight smile tweak its way onto her lips as she thought over just what she had in mind.

Perhaps it would be good news . . . if he was the favourite.

CLEARANCE

1

GREGORY DOONES—or simply *Grey* to his friends—leaned up against the cool metal wall and drummed his calloused fingertips against the surface of the stainless-steel table. The motion made a slight clicking sound. He reached up and ran his fingers over his shaven scalp, and then through his greying, ginger, goatee-styled beard, wondering whether he should've given the beard another pass with the razor that morning. Not that he could've afforded to. Razors didn't simply grow on *trees*, and neither were they manufactured . . . at least not here on Narzook: a planet far, far away from where he called home:

Earth.

He had spent a long time examining himself in the mirror that morning, trying to get his 'look' just right. It'd been a long while since he had got his hands on some new clothes—the Narzook didn't *wear* clothes. He hadn't acquired any new ones since he'd been back on Earth.

Back in that dreary, boxy apartment with his grandmother.

Back in Capital City.

And yet those minor annoyances—his grandmother's perfume, that crushing odour of wilting lilacs which caught in his mouth, and at the back of his throat; the evening after evening lost to babbling TV shows his grandmother only half watched; how his grandmother's cat, Sergreant Strawberries, would claw at his leg if he made even the slightest of unexpected movements—seemed almost immaterial now that he was here on Narzook.

Stuck here on Narzook.

In the end, he had gone with a powder-blue shirt—the one which he judged his *least* creased—and a pair of sensible black jeans which, thanks to Narzook's various gravitational forces he only vaguely understood, would only cling to his waistline under the vigorous guard of a nicely tightened leather belt. He'd gone with a navy-blue, fuzzed-up woolly jumper over the top, and, only five minutes out the door, and with no prospect of returning to change, had already convinced himself that same jumper was a mistake.

He glanced across the table top. He wondered what a place like this might've been called back on Earth. A café? That was probably the closest description.

But there was no service counter—let alone *baristas*—and the only beverages served were those positioned on the standing tables and self-administered by the clientele. He eyed the object which looked remarkably similar to a test tube rack—inspected how each glass vial was filled with a differently coloured liquid:

Silvery-purple.

Mulchy-brown.

Candy-cane pink.

A single, translucent, bendy tube snaked out from the rack.

There was an applicator on the other end of the tube which— as he had often witnessed—was stuck into the throat of the recipient. Whenever he had gone over for social visits with Narzook— those 'integration sessions', as the Cooperative had termed them— he would find himself in that same old embarrassing stalemate, trying to communicate to his host that, really, there was nowhere for said applicator to be applied to.

Not unless their intention was his death.

Some days *that* idea didn't seem too bad.

He glanced at his watch—did the mental acrobatics which were second nature to him now, the ones required to convert the time on his *Earth* watch to Narzook time.

He realised that his date was running late.

Of course she was.

Strange that, although the Narzook bred asexually, he thought of the Narzook coming to meet him as being a 'she' . . . but there it was.

He supposed that even five years down on this rock hadn't been enough to shake him completely out of his human skin.

As he often did when he was waiting, he thought of the last days of the Cooperative. How it'd all run aground so suddenly: six months ago now. The Cooperative's mining permission had been permanently revoked by the Narzook council following some diplomatic row between the Narzook and Humans. Grey—along with his six-strong team—had been left rooted to Narzook with limited to no options for getting off. He and his team had all—extremely *hurriedly*, in Grey's simple opinion—been declared 'unpeople'. Although they had clung to their quarters—the quarters which they'd flown in with them, and settled in just outside Narzook City—finding food, water, or anything else necessary for human survival, had become deeply problematic.

Nonetheless, within the week, the rest of his team had all managed to get themselves off the planet by a variety of means: stowing away on an interstellar container ship; bribing high-ranking Narzook officials with the aid of rich family members back on Earth; or, in one case, doing their very best impression of a Narzook and, somehow—Grey really couldn't comprehend *exactly* how—managing to get themselves promoted to such a level within the spaceport administration that they could then get themselves Clearance as a Narzook citizen.

But none of those was an option for Grey.

For one—being the most senior member of the team, and having a pair of trick knees to contend with—he really couldn't see himself going through with the, no doubt, extremely active motions required of the fledgling stowaway. Second, his family—consisting only of himself and his grandmother—did not possess the means to 'bribe' officials on Narzook, or anywhere else in the universe for that matter. Third of all, Grey was *certain* that his acting ability wouldn't get him even in the door with the Narzook spaceport administration . . . in fact, it was most likely to get him thrown out and executed by whatever grizzly measure the Narzook saw fit.

There was only one option open for Grey now.

And it'd just happened to step through the door.

The force field, to be precise.

Marriage.

2

A LARGE doughy mass—with a colour and consistency much like grape-flavoured jelly—rocked its way toward Grey:

A Narzook.

As she approached—and he was still thinking in terms of *she*—he felt a quivering sensation clench hold of his gut. And refuse to let go.

He forced a smile onto his face and tried to look up at the pinched bundle of goo at the top of the body—the part which Grey liked to think of as the head.

If he squinted *just so*, it was almost as if he was looking at a human body.

As the Narzook drew closer, he caught that stiff, heady stench of sulphur—felt it press itself over his airways. It brought a slight taste of vomit up to the back of his throat.

But he forced himself to swallow it down.

Just like all Narzook, when she walked she made a gentle *thwock-thwock* sound, as if she had been constantly stuck in a swamp, and was desperately trying to break free. She focussed in on him—like all Narzook, she had no eyes, but he could feel the slight tickle as her brainwaves collided with his own. Once more, he wondered if he had been clear enough with his application to the Narzook dating service—after five years here, he would've thought he'd have got around to being able to communicate at a competent level with the Narzook, but he had to admit that his grasp of the Narzook language was pidgin at best. On Narzook, a sort of internet existed as a gigantic network of thoughts, all flung about the planet in a tangled manner . . . well, it seemed 'tangled' to him. Back in his quarters, he had just about managed to get to grips with reading the Narzook internet. This more or less consisted of imagining a series of shapes, bringing to mind certain emotions, and then using those to navigate to some living-breathing part of the internet kept in place by the Narzook thoughts.

If it hadn't been for one of the more competent members of his team—Aina: the one who had managed to pass as Narzook and obtain her Clearance that way—pinning a note with the dating site's Narzook internet location up on the fridge back in their quarters, with the mildly humorous note: 'For a rainy day', then it was quite possible he never would've stumbled across this idea at all.

Smile still pinning his cheeks back, he folded his hands and placed them on the surface of the—suddenly *chilly*—table top. He tilted his head to one side and then, because he couldn't quite manage to communicate without doing so, shut his eyes. He reached out with his mind for the Narzook, did as best as he could to follow all the advice he had been given by the Cooperative so long ago; those tips like ever so gently chewing on the tip of the tongue, and, to begin with, imagining a landscape filled with rolling green hills and burbling fresh-water streams.

This last tip was supposed to keep humans from bringing to mind threatening communications . . . or communications which—to the Narzook—might *seem* threatening.

Grey just about managed to communicate, *Hello, how are you?*

The pause was just long enough so that he managed to half convince himself that he had said something deeply offensive. Right as he was preparing to duck—to sprint from the café, as the Narzook fired its acid spit balls at him—the Narzook replied:

I understand you require Clearance?

Grey felt a little taken aback by the directness.

Not typical of the Narzook by any means.

Second of all, once the directness of the content of the

comment had worn off, he marvelled a little in his ability to understand Narzook at a much higher level than he had anticipated. Usually—even when they spoke slowly to him—it would take a good five, ten seconds before he had deciphered the message within his own brain.

Yes, Grey replied, *I am a human, and I . . .*

Before he could finish, the Narzook interrupted him, *In order to facilitate communication, I am speaking to you in your own language.* There was a brief pause, as if she was giving Grey's —*clearly insufficient*—human brain a chance to catch up with her mind-speak. *I wish to be taken to Earth—to have* Clearance *for Earth.*

Grey opened his eyes. He blinked a couple of times. He knew it had been a mistake for him not to bring his glasses along to this meeting. Already he could feel his eyes straining a little in the harsh, even light of the café. He had thought—again running along *human* terms—that he might appear more attractive *without* the glasses. Now he thought about it, with the Narzook standing across from him, he felt somewhat uncertain about this whole situation. He wondered if this might be some sort of a sting. Did the concept of a 'sting' operation work on Narzook?

If he continued the conversation would a SWAT team—or its Narzook equivalent—leap out from the nooks and crannies of the café and confront him?

The thought was enough to send blood fizzing up into his cheeks.

I took the liberty, the Narzook continued, within the confines of Grey's mind, *of calling in a representative, someone who will be able to offer us guidance.*

"Oh, okay," Grey said, out loud, and even to his own ears sounding a little dim-witted.

I shall call them in now, the Narzook stated, again in Grey's mind.

Sure enough, when he turned his attention to the force field at the entrance of the café, another form stepped through. A *human* form.

He looked to the Narzook. "I, uh, well, I thought that I was the only human here on Narzook?"

The Narzook, apparently understanding his spoken language without any trouble, replied, in his mind, *There is still the Human Embassy.*

Grey shook his head a couple of times as he eyed the approaching woman—dressed in a smart trouser suit, and a pair of well-polished black shoes. She had her hair drawn back in a business-like ponytail and her black hair had a lusty, natural shine to it. She carried a briefcase down at her thigh—*also* black—and, when she arrived at the table, she brought it up and laid it on the surface with smart, no-nonsense precision. She reached up and smoothed the sides of her hair before looking to the Narzook first, and then to Grey, with the briefest flicker of a smile.

To Grey, she reached out to shake his hand.

"Loona Singh. Earth Embassy."

"Uh," Grey said, looking across the table, to the Narzook, then back to Singh, "I thought the Embassy pulled out?"

"No," Singh replied, offering no further explanation as she released his hand and busied herself with her briefcase. For several moments, she bustled about with various electronic devices concealed within.

"But," Grey went on, determined not to let this drop, "when I tried to look up the Embassy—when I found the contact details, went to the Embassy—there was no one there."

"Relocated," Singh said, succinctly, handing an electronic reading device to Grey.

He thought back on that long—*long*—afternoon walking

through Narzook City, the hard, stinging rain coming rattling down on him. The rain which, medical experts had *assured* the Cooperative's mining team before arriving here, was in actual fact harmless. He would've liked to show those 'experts' the burned-in, red rash he now had stretching across his shoulder blades. And how, whenever he took a bite of a cracker—just about the only remaining food item in their quarters which hadn't yet passed its expiry date—he had a faint taste of smoke in his mouth.

And all the way down his throat.

He looked over the text on the screen of the electronic reading device he held in his hand. It might as well have been dozens of black ants—*marching from left to right*—for all the sense it made. He glanced up at the Embassy employee, clearly with a question mark in a bubble floating above his head.

Singh, though, didn't seem to be big on eye contact. She was already busying herself with her own electronic reading device. As she tapped the screen, she said, "It'll be a simple process—nothing out of the ordinary and, if you stick to the plan, there shouldn't be trouble."

Grey looked back down to his reading device, seeing the screens—apparently under Singh's control—dancing about. "What's the plan?" he asked, reading a line of text only for it to shuttle away as the page turned.

Singh stayed quiet and Grey caught a slight sense of tension in the air.

He glanced across the table, to the Narzook opposite, then to Singh again. "Should she have a reader too?"

Not turning her attention away from her reading device, Singh shook her head. "No, I've been relaying all appropriate information through telepathy."

"So you're fluent in Narzook?"

"Uh-huh."

3

GREY FELT a little passenger-like as he observed Singh and the Narzook—*apparently*—speaking to one another through telepathy. Although he could tell that *something* was crackling through the air, and he was able to decode a few words—here and there—he really wouldn't have been able to say that he was in any way *involved* in the conversation.

Leaning against the wall, and feeling cramp working its way slowly from his upper arm all the way down his elbow, he did as he was told. He submitted his biodata to the reader. Answered in the affirmative when asked—in *brisk* terms by Singh—whether or not he agreed to something he really didn't have the foggiest idea about. As the conversation, several hours later, seemed to be reaching an end—Singh was beginning to pack up her suitcase, anyway—he felt increasingly frustrated at being left out of the discussion. Perhaps it was because he had become accustomed to being a leader, to being the senior member of the Cooperative's mining team.

It seemed an awfully long time since he had had anybody to boss around.

"Look here," he said, turning on Singh. "Aren't you going to explain this to me in simple terms, let me know how we're going to make this all work?"

Holding her now-closed briefcase down at her side—the reading devices all nicely snug within—she rolled her eyes ever so slightly.

"If it's not too much trouble," Grey added, in a muttering tone.

"Mr Doones," Singh said, "as far as the Earth Embassy is concerned, our end of the deal is all done. You have now—by the sanctity of *union*—allowed your partner Clearance to Earth."

Grey felt at once a warming and then a cooling sensation pass over his skin. He supposed he should've read those documents he'd agreed to a little more carefully. "We're . . . *married?*"

Singh continued without answering Grey's question. "Although it is out of Earth's jurisdiction to offer advice on the inner workings of Narzook emigration law, your partner has agreed to uphold their end of the bargain—to help you to leave Narzook territory."

With that said, Singh turned to leave, headed for the café force field.

Grey shoved himself away from the wall where he had been leaning and pursued her, determined to get his answers. She wasn't going to brush him off so easily.

Right as Singh was about to cross the threshold, he reached out and grabbed her jacket sleeve. He half expected her to slap him across the face, but, instead, she simply halted and stared at his hand as if it was some minor unpleasantry.

"I don't speak Narzook—I'll happily admit that—but why won't you tell me *how* I'm actually going to get off the planet. What has my *partner* agreed to do?"

For the first time, Singh's lips tweaked into the approximation of an authentic smile.

"*Please?*"

Singh glanced back to the table where Grey's 'partner' still stood. It was as if they were sharing a private joke, through their minds and, as far as Grey knew, they *were*. Singh turned her attention back to Grey. "Really, it's not too difficult, you know?"

"Isn't it? Then would you care to enlighten me?"

"Humans have been afforded a sort of *animal* status here, on Narzook."

"Have they now?"

Singh smiled wider.

His heart beat faster.

Perhaps this *was* all a setup after all—perhaps the Narzook authorities were just waiting to pounce.

Singh went on, "What your partner has agreed to do is to carry you through emigration as a pet."

"A 'pet' ?" Grey replied.

"Yes, however, due to several interspecies regulations—lots of details I wouldn't *dream* of boring you with—you'll be considered by Earth as an extra-terrestrial specimen and be subject to quarantine."

" '*Quarantine*' !" Grey said, unable to keep his anger from bubbling to the surface now.

His hold on Singh's sleeve closed in tighter.

"But I'm *human*," he added.

Singh gave a nonchalant shrug, glanced back over to the table where the Narzook waited, gave a smile and then, wiping same smile off her face, turned to Grey. "If you'd just let me go, I'll allow you to go about your business."

Grey, though, continued to hold her sleeve tightly. He realised he was shaking his head, from side to side, unable to quite believe what he had heard. " 'Quarantine' ," he repeated. "For how *long?*"

"The standard period is six months—up to two years if required."

" '*Two years*' ?"

Singh nodded and then slipped herself free of Grey's grasp.

Grey no longer had the strength to take hold of her a second time.

"It's quite nice," Singh went on, "from what I've heard—space station, orbiting Earth."

"But I'll be in a *cage!*"

Again, Singh gave a shrug. "You'll have some nice kibble and your water bowl will be kept disinfected, I would imagine."

He gave her a *stony* stare. "Do you find this funny?"

She shrugged, then gave him a slight smile. "Humour can be hard to come by on Narzook. You've got to take what you can get." With that, she disappeared through the force field.

Grey stood still, feeling as if his brain was swelling up. He glanced back to the table, where his partner awaited him. Saw that —in what he supposed served as a *hand*—she held a dog collar.

And a chain.

As he shifted back off in the direction of the table—for some fresh humiliation—he wondered if Singh had surreptitiously left those items behind.

OTHER LIVES

1

S TANLEY SMITH twisted his key in the lock to his front door and then stepped out along his garden path, heading for the bus stop and another day at work. He checked his watch and, seeing it had just gone ten past eight, increased his pace.

A man with a grey beard and murky-green tweed jacket strolled with his head propped back, whistling tunelessly.

Stanley bustled into him, apologised and then hurried on.

The man called something after him, but Stanley didn't hear.

As he turned the corner he caught sight of the bus pulling out of the bay and resuming its journey up the main road into town.

Stanley broke into a run, his briefcase slapping against his thigh. He screamed and shouted after the bus but, if anything, it accelerated. After another few seconds, he gave up the chase, dropped his briefcase in frustration and stomped his foot.

Once he got himself under control, he checked his watch again. Eight fifteen. It would be another fifteen minutes before the next bus passed. If he took that one he would be late for work. If there was one thing which he valued above all else it was that he arrived on time every morning. His boss had praised the matter in his last performance review. And he had no intention of letting anyone down, of busting their slick and spotless image of Stanley Smith.

He whipped his mobile phone out of his pocket and dialled up a taxi firm. The line burbled on hold. He tapped his foot, checked his watch again. Eight twenty now. After what seemed an eternity, a voice answered, he gave them his details and they sent a taxi right away.

Another frustrating wait before the taxi arrived. A dark, well-polished estate. He clambered into the back seat and instructed the driver on his destination. The car twirled and wound along the country lanes, brushing overgrown grassy banks.

Eight thirty.

At this rate he would arrive before nine, with a few minutes to spare, his reputation in tact. In fact he would arrive earlier than usual. They must have overtaken the bus on their way.

At eight forty-five they struck morning rush hour. An endless tailback of cars queuing to enter into the city. Stanley tapped his fingers against his briefcase, as if the hollow sound might sooth his aching nerves.

Twenty years. Never a day off ill. Never a day late.

The green LED clock on the taxi driver's dashboard struck eight forty-seven.

With a swish, the bus ploughed by them through its exclusive red-marked lane.

Stanley's final resolve cracked. "Follow that bus!"

The driver frowned at him in the rear view mirror. "More than my job's worth, mate."

The clock ticked over to eight fifty.

Stanley examined the interior of the car, feeling it close in on him, tighten around his throat. It was difficult to breath. He choked on the stale air.

The driver pivoted in his seat. "You all right? You've gone all pale."

"Let me out here!"

"Okay, that'll be fourteen seventy."

Hands shaking, Stanley passed him a twenty note. The red light indicating the secure doors blinked off and the locks snapped open. He leapt out of the car and bustled his way through the stationary traffic, up onto the pavement, and he was running.

Sweat rolled down his face. It tasted salty on his lips. He bounded along the path, his tie flapping over his shoulder. As if to mock him, another bus swooshed by in its dedicated lane. He chased after it, knowing full well that he had to arrive at the office before it did. That bus would arrive after nine.

Eight fifty-three.

Stanley eyed an alley and sprinted for it without another second's consideration. He splashed through puddles and clods of mud clung to the soles of his shoes. He increased his pace, slipped and slid onto his knees through manky-brown puddles. The stench of dog crap and earth clawed his nostrils. He picked himself up and ran on.

He emerged into a side street and lost his way for a moment. He dared not pause to checked his surroundings. Every heartbeat was another wasted.

Finally he arrived on the street where his office was located. His soiled trousers stuck to his legs. The acquired odours mingled with his clean sweat, oozing lime shower gel. He noticed a rip in his jacket, a frayed section of his lapel.

Eight fifty-eight.

Stanley barrelled along, knocking a passer-by into the wall. A barrage of swear words drifted in his wake but he ignored them and stumbled on. His office's placard filled his vision: Olive Investments and Loans.

Eight fifty-nine.

He reached the front door of the building. He stabbed his finger at the scanner. It glowed green and the lock buzzed back. He shoved it open.

The lift was out of order so he trotted up the stairs, taking them three at a time. He arrived at his office on the fifth floor. He eyed the chrome clock on the wall as it clicked over to nine o'clock. He allowed himself a broad grin as he strolled in.

Mission accomplished.

Jenny Adams, the secretary, eyed him over her desk. Her

eyebrows rose and her lips parted. "My goodness, Stan, whatever happened to you?"

Adrenalin dripped from his veins, like a clockwork toy winding itself down. He gulped air and tried to refind his poise and dignity. He glanced over his torn and tattered suit.

Jenny held her hand over her mouth and nose. "It smells of . . . of dog poo."

As if he hadn't noticed, Stanley gave himself a sniff. He retched.

"You'd better go get cleaned up."

Stanley looked himself over once more, still wondering quite what had come over him, how he had ended up in this state. "Yes, I'd better."

Jenny stared at him as he slunk over to the toilets.

The contrast between the disinfectant and the dog crap was dizzying. He checked himself in the mirror, observing the damage. As a rule he bought a work suit once every year. The thirty-first of March, always. This suit had hardly lasted six months.

He entered one of the cubicles and wiped himself down as best he could with a damp paper towel. When he had got the worst of the crap off he observed himself in the mirror once more. He gave his face a quick wash and then made for his desk.

As he gazed over his hundred-odd emails his whole mind phased out, got away from him. He looked away from his screen, tried to rethread the ripped edges of his mind and resume his work.

He doubled over in his chair and pressed the heels of his hands into his eyes, trying to shake the sensation. His whole body shook. He felt numb and empty. He slumped back in his chair, staring up at the perfectly square, bleached-white ceiling panels.

Alan, his co-worker in the next workstation along, peeked over the top of his terminal. "You all right there, Stan?"

Stanley flinched and fixed his glare on him.

Alan cracked a smile. "Look like you've had a rough night."

"Nah." Stanley swallowed. "No, a rough morning."

Alan leant closer, sniffed. His eyes darted in their sockets. "You . . . you haven't been drinking, have you, Stan?"

"No drinking, no."

"Then are you feeling well? Got a headache or something?"

"No."

Alan withdrew behind his computer.

Stanley pressed his fingers to his temples, making the circular motions as he had been taught in a training session aimed at reducing work stress. He sat there massaging himself for several minutes. His brain buzzed and twitched. He was afraid sparks might fly from his ears. But after a while he felt much better, more under control.

What was it? Was he fed up with his life? Tired and stretched from this in out, eight hours a day, five hours a week, twenty years? Perhaps. That would be understandable.

Everyone else, though, they all got on with it. Acted like rational human beings. Could he not do the same? He experimented, pulled himself back up to his computer monitor on his wheeled chair. His eyes blurred once more and his capacity for reading disappeared. The words marched back and forth, left to right, a battalion of black ants.

He reached for his keyboard. His arms lost control and his hand slapped it, mashed the keys.

Alan glanced up over his monitor, eyes wide. "Stan, shall I got get help? Call a doctor?"

Stanley crunched his teeth, tried to seize control of the tremors consuming his body. He made his fingers crooked, forced them down onto the keyboard. He felt the plastic keys, the springs pushing up at his fingertips as if they shoved him away.

His eyes felt like a pair of pulsating bull testicles. His nostrils flapped.

Alan got up from his station and called out, over the office.

The words only reached Stanley as muffled, muted screams. He glowered at his screen, its irradiated light. His whole world burst at the seems. Molecules trickled in around the edges, whizzing past him, smashing into one another, tickling him all over.

And then it all retreated. The jagged frontiers returned. The world came into focus. The emails made sense once more. He could read. He could control his limbs. He reached for his mouse, still trembling a touch, and clicked on the first. Yes! He could do this.

He rested back in his chair and wondered at re-finding himself.

Footsteps scrunched over the coarse beige carpet. His name. "Stanley? Stanley? Stan?"

Stanley turned in his chair, a smile now pressed firmly onto his lips.

Alan stood alongside Nick, his boss. Both of them wore expressions of concern.

Nick stepped forward and laid a hand on Stanley's shoulder. "Alan told me all about it." He glanced back, as if for confirmation. "Would you like me to call an ambulance?"

A new sense of lightness entered Stanley's being. He clasped his hands over his belly, feeling the smooth skin on the sides of his fingers brush together. "I'm quite all right now."

"You're still really pale," Alan said.

Nick whisked out his mobile phone. "Yes, I'd better call an ambulance."

Fifteen minutes later, after the paramedics had examined Stanley and delivered a clean bill of health, Nick attempted to send him home for the day, but Stanley refused. He did, however, nip out at lunchtime to buy a new suit.

That afternoon he slid a cup into the appropriate slot of the coffee machine and returned to his tasks. All this drama had meant him getting behind on his emails and so he plunged into them with a vengeance: declining, approving, diverting, summarising. And all through the day he kept up his routine, performing whatever tasks Nick dished out to him.

By five o'clock most people in the office had forgotten about his episode earlier in the day. He reflected on this fact as he shrugged on his overcoat and headed for the exit.

On his way out he met Jenny's eye and smiled.

She smiled back, still with a glimmer of wariness.

He bid her a good evening and clumped down the staircase with his briefcase at his side. As he reached the plateau of another floor he noticed a light scuff mark on its side. He disregarded it, promising himself that he would take care of it later that evening— make sure that tomorrow everything would go just as he intended it to. And that he would once again be the ever dependable and unshakable employee that he had always been.

Stanley Smith. Straight as an arrow, clear thinking and logical. That was the name he had made for himself and he would be damned if anyone or anything would get in its way.

Back down on the street he waited the customary eleven minutes before his bus arrived. He stuck out his arm and boarded.

2

G RAVEL CRUNCHED beneath his feet as he trudged up the driveway to his front door. As he meshed his key into the lock. He paused. From within he heard laughter. The clanging of pots and pans.

Intruders. He should call the police. He backed up from the door and whisked out his mobile phone. He had hardly brought the speaker to his ear when the door squeaked open.

A slim woman with silky-blond hair and a pearl-coloured top, which plunged downward to reveal a crevice of cleavage. She rested her knuckle on her hip. "Thought I heard your key. What's the matter? Who're you calling?"

Stanley's heart throbbed in his ears. Someone spoke on the other end of the phone line. He hung up. "Who are you?"

She raised an eyebrow. "Mary. Wife of seven years. Remember me?"

Before Stanley had a chance to respond, to ask this stranger what she was doing in his house, footsteps scuffled over the hall carpet and two blurred figures flew into his stomach. "Daddy!" the two children, a boy and a girl, said.

Their little hands curled themselves around his thighs, their fingernails digging into his trousers and pressing up against his flesh.

"Uh, uh," Stanley said.

Mary rolled her eyes and smiled. She beckoned him inside. "Come on, Mr Joker, dinner's almost ready."

The children snatched hold of his hands and dragged him over the hearth and into his house. It was his house, wasn't it?

Onions and spices stunk out the kitchen. Stanley observed in wonder the stove in use. The microwave, which he used to heat his ready meals every night, stood to one side, covered in a layer of dust. The children released him and tramped into the sitting room. He strode up to his fridge and cranked open the freezer compartment. No ready meals there either. What in hell's name was this place?

Mary stirred away at the pot on the stove. It bubbled away and steam rose in the air. She had the extractor fan going. Another first for his house. In fact he had forgotten it had existed. Without turning round she said, "Take a seat, dear. You look exhausted."

Shaking all over, Stanley drew back one of the chairs. It was make of heavy wood, unlike the light-weight ones he had bought as temporary measures, when he had moved into the house, and never got round to replacing. He took a seat, wondering what would happen when the real man returned home here, found him at his kitchen table. But this was his house. These people were the intruders.

"So how was your day?" she said.

"Uh, uh . . . I . . ."

She turned, glanced him over and pouted. "You look a little pale. Are you sure you're feeling quite all right?"

"It's . . . uh, just, a . . . erm."

She trotted over to the kitchen sink and poured him a glass of water, which she handed to him.

He took deep gulps, feeling the liquid sooth his hot, dry throat.

She crouched down and fumbled open a cupboard, from which she withdrew a stack plates. She laid them on the kitchen surface, beside the stove and dished out steaming sauce onto spaghetti.

"Today . . . uh . . . in the office. Something happened."

She set the wooden spoon down in the pan, faced him and frowned.

"Like the whole world broke apart. I dunno."

"What're you talking about, Stan?"

He inspected his suit and noticed it was spotless. There was no trace of his rush to work that morning. He lost the thread of the conversation and looked up at her with a wrinkled brow. "Huh?"

Mary's nose twitched. "Dear, maybe you should go and lie down."

Stanley realised he was famished. He would eat first and ask questions later. "I'll be all right. I think I'm just hungry." He attempted a smile. "Really."

"Okay," she said, returning to serving out the plates.

Once the plates lay smouldering on the table, Mary called to the children who plodded back down and bombed in through the kitchen. They took up their seats, both of them grinning as if they shared a secret between them.

Had they realised that he was an imposter?

They tucked into their dinner without conversation. He supposed this to be the normal order of things and so followed suit. He noticed Mary glance up from her plate and give him an anxious glance. He did his best to focus on his dinner, getting it down him. Everything made more sense on a full stomach.

After they'd finished, the children scattered out of the kitchen, back up the stairs. Mary collected up the dishes and rinsed them in the sink, before slotting them into the dishwasher.

He stared, transfixed.

Mary bumped the dishwasher door shut and it trundled into action. She met his eye. "What? What is it?"

"I . . . I don't know who you are."

She brought her hand up to her forehead and slumped into the seat opposite him. "This isn't a joke, is it?"

He shook his head.

"Did you hit your head? Something like that?"

"Maybe." He paused. "No."

"Then what?" she said, her tone hardening. "Tell me what happened."

"It's impossible to explain. I had just arrived to work on time."

She scoffed. "On time? I can't remember the last time you managed to get there before nine thirty. No matter what you do you always end up missing the bus because you wait for the children to get theirs first."

"Does . . . doesn't anyone mind about me arriving late?"

"No, they know you have kids. Nick's your best mate. His wife's mine. They have kids too, they understand what it's like. Some things are more important than work."

"Uh huh."

She wriggled her nose and blinked a couple of times. "I'm going to call a doctor, Stan. It might be that you knocked your head on something." She scooted over to the landline, plucked it from its base.

"Wait."

"What is it?"

"At the office. After my . . . my attack. They had an ambulance come. The paramedic checked me over. He said I was fine."

"Well, maybe they missed something."

"You may be right."

She held a hushed conversation with the doctor on the other end of the line. Once she had finished she replaced the phone and approached him. "They say that you should go down to Accident and Emergency immediately."

"I don't want to cause a fuss."

Her eyeballs bulged in their sockets. "Men: it's always the same. Squeamish about doctors." She gave him a sly grin. "Don't worry, they're not going to cut your balls off or anything."

Mary collected together the children and packed them all into an estate car they kept in the garage. It was a boxy shape and had a sweet smell of caramel and neutral car odour.

As Stanley clipped his seatbelt into place he considered the fact that this wasn't his car. He had never owned a car. Didn't even have a license.

Mary slipped him a sideways glance. "You don't remember this either, do you?"

"No. I can't drive."

Sighing, she turned the ignition and released the handbrake. "Tell me about it. Sometimes it feels like I'm a designated driver for life."

It took about quarter of an hour to arrive at the hospital. Mary parked up and they headed for the hospital. One of the children, the girl, perked up. "Is Daddy poorly, Mummy?"

"We don't know," Mary said.

The girl tweaked one of her plaits, flicked it over her shoulder. "Is the doctor going to give him medicine?"

"Maybe."

The boy clutched Stanley's hand.

A flush of warmth passed through him, like no other sensation he had felt. Something within him told him that this boy was his. When he examined his face he noted the similar dopey eyes, the square jaw and nose bent a touch to the left.

They swept in through the sliding doors and took up their places to await triage. The flickering fluorescent lights made Stanley's head fizz. A hint of the sensation he had experienced earlier that day, at his desk.

The doctors ordered an MRI scan and Stanley complied with everything asked of him, donning a hospital gown and performing various tests. After several hours the doctors announced that they could find nothing wrong with him. They discharged him and handed over a number of a psychiatrist.

Mary broke into tears.

A hollowness opened up within Stanley's chest. Although he had no doubt this woman was attractive, and that he felt sorry for her tears, there was no stirring within him. No love. When her glossy, tearful eyes closed in on his she saw that too. And a deadness consumed everything.

On the car ride home the children slept, their little toy faces a pair of miniature mixtures of their parents.

Stanley faced forward, terrified of unlocking his gaze from the streaking white lines flowing past, like a chalked river. He locked his fingers together and squeezed, testing to see whether he was dreaming. He didn't wake up.

When they returned home Mary bathed the children, read them a goodnight story, meanwhile, Stanley sat at the kitchen table, staring at the microwave, knowing that it was part of his life, and that he had no wife or children. He had never married, let alone had kids. Of that he was one hundred per cent certain.

He listened to Mary's footsteps pad along the landing, open the bedroom door and close it behind her with a solid, earthy *click*. He remained where he was, lost in a sea of thought and tribulation. Tomorrow he would return to work, be back at his computer. Perhaps then it would all return to him. His past life would come back.

And then he thought over his situation. His wife and children, tiny copies of himself. Hadn't that been what he had wanted his whole life? At the back of everything hadn't he regretted never having found someone on his level, who he might be able to share life with? He supposed that he had never believed in any other form of variables. The life he had chosen to live had been the one and only. What had defined Stanley Smith.

After a long period of rhetorical questions and internal discussion, he climbed the stairs, shifted up to his bedroom and slipped inside.

Weak perfume trailed up his nostrils. He undressed in the darkness, listening to the sound of Mary's gentle and rhythmic breathing. He knew she wasn't sleeping.

Another moment's hesitation and then he sat on the edge of the bed, pushed back the sheet and got into the bed beside her. They lay there, both deathly still, sharing body heat.

And then Mary rested her head on his chest. Their breathing mingled into one and Stanley slipped into sleep.

S TANLEY WAS BACK where he had started. His head spun. He rocked himself back into a sitting position. Clammy fingers pressed his skin. He gazed up.

Nick and Alan bore down on him, their lips jabbering and cheeks pinched.

Stanley looked from one to the other, realising he was right back where he had started. Although he still felt shaky, he managed a smile. "It's okay, I'm fine."

"You sure?" Alan said. "Your eyes were spinning around."

Nick whisked out his phone and dialled. "I'm calling an ambulance."

Stanley had no wish to fight back. He knew the outcome. He waited for the paramedics, got checked over. As they did so, Jenny, the receptionist, stood over him her eyes darting him, her head turning to listen in on every word the doctor said. When the doctor finished, she gave Stanley a slither of a smile and skulked back off to the reception.

With a clean bill of health, Stanley bid the paramedics goodbye then slumped back in his chair. Perhaps his wife and children had all been a dream, while he'd been knocked out. This was his real life. He was back where he belonged. He was sure of it. And then he caught sight of the photographs lining his cubicle wall.

Photographs he had never seen. There was one of his and Mary's wedding. Mary looked incredible in her lily-white dress, her china cheeks glinting in the sunlight. Stanley too was beaming, and he noted how he appeared to have dropped several kilogrammes. He looked much younger, more vital. He supposed kids and work had aged him.

Another photograph featured his children dressed up for Halloween. The girl was dressed up as a ballerina, or a princess, with frilly pink lace and a tiara perched in her tangled mousy hair. The boy wore a superhero costume with a foam six-pack and biceps. Both smiled for the camera. He wondered whether he had taken that photograph.

It had all been real then. He had woken up here, in the same situation, and he was still stuck here. Or had his old life ever really been real? Was he just in the midst of a horrible breakdown?

During the afternoon, as he shifted from one task to the next, he considered his situation. All things considered, he was doing much better than he had been in his previous life—whatever that had been, when he had left his house that morning, or was it yesterday morning? He now had a beautiful wife, children. Actual living breathing people in his house. Hadn't he somewhere, at the back of his mind, wanted that?

Whatever had happened to him today, yesterday, he was determined to set things right and to be on his way in this new, improved life. He had no doubts about what to do. When he finished up work today he would go back home, ruffle his children's hair—he really had to learn their names—and then he would kiss his wife, long and passionately. Afterward he would apologise for his behaviour, make peace with Mary. Maybe even learn to love her.

Stanley bustled through his workload, glancing at the clock every couple of minutes. Finally it reached five o'clock, he pulled on his overcoat and wandered for the stairwell. On his way out he heard a shrill wolf whistle. He glanced back.

Jenny leant over her desk with a smirk on her lips. A strong scent of flower blossoms wafted over. "Where do you think you're going?"

"Uh, home."

"Home?"

"Yeah." He glanced at his watch. "Don't want to be late for dinner."

She batted her eyelashes and then pawed her black hair out of her glimmering green eyes. "You can't go home."

Stanley's muscles tautened. "What? Why?"

"Because your wife chucked you out, remember?"

Stanley grasped his briefcase handle tighter. "Uh, really?"

"Yuh."

He peered down the stairs, wondering whether she was telling the truth, if someone was playing a trick on him. Maybe they had set up hidden cameras. Soon a presenter would dive out from behind the scenery. But who would want him on their show? Boring old, predictable Stanley Smith?

Jenny twisted a strand of hair around her forefinger. She bowed her head and shot him a slender look. "What happened today, Stan?"

"I . . . I had a headache, just felt faint for a moment."

She rested back in her chair and her eyes wandered over him. "You're all right, aren't you? I mean, the doctor said that he couldn't find anything wrong."

"I feel fine."

"Good," she said, breaking out into another smile.

Stanley moved his weight from one foot to the other. "I know this will sound weird, but where do I live?"

She snorted. "You sure you're all right, Stan?"

"Yeah."

"You"—her tone of voice dipped and she leant closer—"still want me to come over tonight?"

Blood pumped to his temples. "Uh, okay."

"Good." She sank back in her seat. "I've got some stuff to finish up. Shall we say seven?"

"O—okay."

She furrowed her brow. "You sure you'll be all right on the way home? Not going to topple over again, are you?"

"No, no, I'll be okay."

She grinned, showing off a perfect horseshoe of cream teeth.

He lingered at the top of the stairs, made to step down and then turned back to her. "You couldn't just write my address, could you? I . . . I know this sounds silly but I'd like to take a taxi. And I can't for the life of me remember it. Haven't had anything sent there, never needed to know."

She stared at him, narrowed her eyes and cocked her head. With a slight smile she reached down under the reception desk and whisked out a pad of paper. "Who are you and what have you done to Stanley Smith?"

Stanley's blood froze.

She cackled then scrawled down the address, tore off the slip and handed it to him. "Here you go, Douglas Quail."

"Thanks," Stanley said, taking the paper. "It's . . . it's just I feel a little dizzy. Like my brain's not quite in full gear. Got a lot on my mind."

"Yeah, Stan, I can see that." Her smile faded and she resumed her anxious expression. "Phone me if you need anything, okay? I'll be over in a couple of hours."

Stanley made his way down the stairs, trying to put all the pieces in order. His children, his house, his wife, all of those had been taken from him, in a fell swoop. He had lost everything before he had realised exactly what it was that he had.

On the street he considered heading back to his house, confronting Mary. But he had no idea what they had been through together, what had caused the split. Could it have been Jenny? That seemed the sensible solution. And why did he keep up his and Mary's wedding photograph in his cubicle. The best course of action was to make for the address which Jenny had given him. He could lie low and think things through for a while.

So he hailed a passing cab and got into the back seat.

Twenty minutes later the driver pulled up at the curb of a block of flats. He asked Stanley if this were the place, to which he replied in the affirmative. He paid him and then remembered the piece of paper. When he requested it back, the driver gave him a funny look, but passed it over. Stanley made some remark about recycling and then stepped out.

Holding the paper in his sweating palm he skirted the periphery. The flats piled up three storeys high. They were rectangular with fawn walls and dirty white doors. He supposed this was a temporary measure, that the separation with Mary had occurred suddenly and this was the only place he could find at such short notice. He was searching for number thirty-six. He hopped up the staircase, to the third storey and examined the numbers.

Number thirty-six stood at the end of the row. He patted his coat pocket, finding a large, heavy key there. It was the sort of key which opened rusty treasure troves but he doubted anything beyond the ordinary lay on the other side of the door. Still, he turned the key and went in.

The curtains were drawn, setting the place in a kind of perpetual twilight. He flipped on the light switch. A bare bulb dazzled the room, as if slapping it awake. There was a gas stove shoved up against one wall, a vase of wilting flowers on the counter beside it. A sofa bed and a large grey CRT television occupied the other wall. Aside from these items there was a door, which he believed led to a bathroom. It reminded him of a seedy motel room, which it might well have been at some time in the past.

As he crept further into the room an odour of rotten apples dampened his nostrils. His foot kicked an empty bottle and it clinked over the floor. Cider.

He stood steeped in the room, letting its oppressiveness wash over him, and then he set his briefcase down, shucked his coat and took a shower.

In a wardrobe positioned behind the television he located his suits, shirts and trousers, all just about packed into the cosy space. He pulled out a polo shirt and a pair of jeans, his clothes he recognised from home, and then he settled on the edge of the sofa to think things through.

In the midst of his thoughts he heard footsteps tramp their way along the walkway outside and then pause outside his door. A pair of short, sharp knocks.

He flinched and then leapt to his feet. He clicked open the lock.

Jenny stood there, still dressed in her work clothes, her jacket draped over her arm. She had tied her hair back and her cheeks looked rosier. He realised she had applied more make up. "Well, don't just leave a girl standing on the doorstep, will you?" She shoved her jacket at him.

Bemused, he took it and hung it over his own, hanging off the back of a frail plastic chair that would've been more at home in a garden.

Jenny closed the door behind her and lunged forward into his arms. She kissed his neck and her hands clawed at his shoulder blades and then moved down his back.

The air seeped from Stanley's lungs, like a slit bellows. He prised her away.

"What?" she said, glaring. "What is it?"

"I . . . I can't."

"What do you mean, 'you can't?' We've been doing this for years. You told me so many times you would leave her." She broke into a grin. "And then you did." She stepped back toward him. "It's us, only us now. No one in between." She reached to touch his chest but he backed away.

Stanley's brain bucked and bolted. All of a sudden it was clear. He had to go to his wife, to Mary, whatever had gone wrong he had to put it right. No way could he be here, not with Jenny, not when he had a wife and children, a family.

He made for the door but Jenny stepped into his path.

"Where in hell's name are you going?" she said.

"H—home."

"Oh, no. You're not going back there." She dug her fingernails into her scalp, combing her smooth coffee-coloured hair. "You made your choice. You chose me!"

A neighbour shouted, "Shut up!" through the thin wall.

"Sorry," Stanley replied, dodging Jenny and unclipping the door.

Jenny broke into fits of screaming. She lashed out at him. Flecks of spittle collected on Stanley's collar.

Stanley slipped outside, onto the walkway.

The vase of wilting flowers whistled over his head and smashed in the car park below.

Stanley broke into a run. He leapt down the stairs and then rushed out of the block of flats, brushing the chain-link fence which surrounded the compound. He dashed into the road and into the path of a lorry, which ran him down.

4

AFTER THE PARAMEDICS had checked him over, Stanley leant back in his chair and tried to figure out what the hell was going on. He peered around the office at the others busily tapping away at their keyboards, already forgetting what they had just witnessed.

Stanley hooked his overcoat off the back of his chair and strolled out of the office. No one tried to stop him. When he passed by the reception desk Jenny gave him a sliver of a smile before returning to her computer screen and he knew that nothing more offensive than a courteous greeting had passed between the two of them.

At that time the bus was almost empty so he relished finding a seat. There was no traffic either so the bus whizzed along the long roads back toward his house. He stared out the window, heart thumping in his ears, wondering what in hell's name he could expect next.

When the bus pulled up at the stop, he got down, his fingers tightening around his briefcase handle and sweat dampening the collar of his shirt. All he wanted was to find his house as it was, had been, and go on living his life. He decided that if he found it as it was he could put all that happened behind him, return to work and finish out his day.

He crunched up the gravel drive and stuck his key in the door. It turned and he stepped inside. He closed the door behind him and stood in the silent hall, savouring the feeling being back in his house, alone. Almost impossible to believe.

He set his briefcase down at his feet and allowed the tension to seep out of his shoulders.

Deep within the house a woman said, "Marty is that you?"

Stanley's heart sank. He parted his lips to reply but before he could the woman appeared at the top of the staircase.

She glared down at him, head cocked slightly to one side. "Who . . . who are you?"

"Just wait a minute—"

She let loose a scream.

It pierced Stanley's ears and sent his pulse rattling in his ears. His nerves knotted and his head felt like a damp, wrung rag. He swept up his briefcase, disengaged the door latch and bolted.

He jogged on down the road until he reached the park nearby. He slowed to a walk and paced his way over to one of the benches where he sat to catch his breath.

A pair of mums supervised their children running about the playground. They held their arms across their chests, while the children's high-pitched voices twinkled in the afternoon air.

Stanley ran his hands through his hair and released a great sigh. He crocked his head back, resting it against the hard wood, and stared upward into the azure sky, losing himself in the impossibility and largeness of the universe. This was his little corner, though, right? This was his world. If that were true, then what was going on? Everything had upped and changed on him, like he'd gone off to the toilet and returned to find all inexplicably rearranged.

He sat there on the bench, letting his vision go fuzzy, the blue sky and the green grass to meld into one another. His brain felt hot and molten. Should he go to the hospital? But he had already gone with Mary. Had that really happened?

Tears of unease and confusion prickled the corners of his eyes. They rolled heavy down his cheeks, wetting his skin and making him sniff. He stared at his briefcase, propped at the foot of the bench. He snatched it up, laid it down on his lap and then flipped the catches. The hinge swung open with a *creak*.

Full of paper. White paper. Nothing written on it.

Fingers quivering, he dug through the papers, feeling them slip through his fingers. They flurried up around him and sailed away in the breeze. He watched them disperse in all directions, like a thousand minute seagulls.

The paper drifted over to the mothers. The children jigged around, laughing and clapping, snatching the paper out of the air and crunching it in their fists.

Not bothering to close up his briefcase, leaving it lying opened on his lap, Stanley pressed his warm, moist palms into his eyes and sobbed on.

Maybe he sat there seconds, perhaps minutes or hours. He heard the squelch of footfall passing over the soggy ground and then pausing before him. He wiped his face on the sleeve of his suit sleeve and peered upward.

A blond police officer loomed over him. His face was thrown into shadow and his features were no more than rutted representations of a nose, eyes and mouth. His lips moved to speak but the words tangled in the air and never reached Stanley's ears. Before long the officer was shaking him by the shoulder, bringing his face closer to Stanley's. The officer's pitted eye sockets widened and infuriated of their own will.

Stanley felt himself tugged to his feet. His body lightened and his feet felt like feathers, merely tickling the earth below him.

The officer wrenched Stanley's hands behind his back and locked them in place with a pair of handcuffs. He shoved him forward, across the park, passed the bemused mothers and children watching on as Stanley was taken away.

Stanley hardly noticed as the officer helped him into the back of the car, dropping his briefcase on the seat beside him, slamming the door. He looked back over his shoulder, into the sky, where the papers continued to rise into the sky. Soon they would be with the clouds.

He noticed another officer sitting up front. The two officers remained silent throughout the journey, like a pair of mannequins, tilting and swaying along with the motion of the car.

When they reached the station, Stanley put up no fight against the officers as they escorted him in through the hallway, past the officer waiting at the desk and then into a backroom where they set him down on a flimsy plastic chair and eyeballed him.

Stanley couldn't stop his head from lolling forward onto his chest.

One of the officers called for a jug of water and some glasses. They arrived a matter of moments later.

As Stanley sipped at his water from a plastic cup he felt his senses partially restored. He caught a hold of himself and the world cleared up somewhat. The officers faces unknitted themselves from all-consuming shadow and sharpened themselves into an approximation of human features.

Both officers remained standing, one at the door, the other, the blond one, bearing down on him, his hands set on the table and mouth wobbling in hyperactive motion. The words cleared up, unjumbled, ". . . and so tell us, sir, what exactly did you think you were doing?"

Stanley looked from one officer to the other, trying to ascertain the seriousness of the situation. He wished to put his dilemma to the men, what had happened to him. He was sure that if he got a hold of himself, put on a reasonable tone, they would listen to him and he could get them to understand his confusion, his side of things.

But when he opened his mouth to speak his tongue welted and he blabbered.

The officers narrowed their eyes at him. The blond one turned side on and talked in a hushed tone with the other. Their shoulders hunched and relaxed while their eyes and noses seemed to bob around their faces, like icebergs on a melting arctic sea.

The blond officer looked back to Stanley. His expression had transformed from one of intimidation to another of deep concern. His lips were flapping again. ". . . is there anyone we can call for you, sir?"

Blood pumped into Stanley's cheeks. It spiralled around his mouth and tasted like rust. He swallowed several times but couldn't lose the sensation. He nodded several times.

The officers exchanged glances once more, and the other, standing at the door, slipped out and down the corridor.

The blond officer took up the seat opposite and stared at him, fingers drumming on the metal table. He continued to speak but, seeing that Stanley wouldn't reply, he gave up after a few minutes and sat back in the chair, not daring to take his eyes off him.

The other officer returned with a doctor, in any case he wore a stethoscope around his neck. The doctor checked over Stanley, measuring his heart rate, beat and his blood pressure. Seemingly satisfied, he slunk out of the room the same way he had come.

Stanley passed another long period in the room with the blond officer. Although he realised that he should make small talk he was simply unable. Those papers, flying upward into the sky stayed with him, forever scarred into his brain tissue.

Finally, the door opened once more, and a familiar face, escorted by the other officer, entered the room. It was Nick, his boss.

Nick swooped down on Stanley, laying his hand on his shoulder. Nick always knew just what he had to say. He smiled and spoke quickly to the officers, who nodded back at him, shooting the occasional glance at Stanley, giving him slight grins.

Finally Nick gripped Stanley around the arm and helped him

up from his chair. Together they walked along the winding corridors, escorted by the blond officer, and into the car park where Nick's brand-new, well-polished company car awaited them. He helped Stanley into the passenger side before getting in himself.

For Stanley, the journey flew by without much impact. The darkened roads, orange streetlights and crescent moon glowing through the clouds, like a light bulb through netted curtains, dusted with cobwebs.

They arrived at Nick's house, which Stanley had visited a handful of times over the years, for work barbeques, the annual Christmas drinks party. Nick helped Stanley out of the car and up, over the front step and into his living room.

After a long time of Nick looking at him, with his hand resting on Stanley's knee, Stanley managed to get out a word. "Help."

Nick smiled. "You're okay now, Stan, don't worry."

A female face appeared in the doorway. Nick's wife. She wore a beige dressing gown and clutched a tray bearing a steaming hot bowl and mug. She brought it in and laid it down on a table, before slinking back out again, managing another glance over her shoulder at Stanley.

"Should have told me, Stan," Nick said, his features blurring a little around the edge. "Should have told me."

Stanley just nodded in response. When he attempted to smile an irrepressible itching broke out around his mouth and so he stopped. He stared back into Nick's eyes, telling himself that if he just kept looking that everything would return to him—that the world would put itself back into order, the right order.

Under Nick's watchful gaze, Stanley ate his way through the soup and sipped at the hot chocolate. The food had no effect on him, did nothing to exorcise the dizziness and nausea surging through his system, wreaking havoc on his internal organs, squeezing them like sponges. But he held himself together.

Nick showed him up to the guest room and had him lie down on the bed. He said several more things before he closed the door and left Stanley alone.

Stanley lay back on his pillow and stared up through the ceiling window, up to the crescent moon in the sky above and he thought over those several pieces of paper and whether they might've reached it by now. He decided it would be impossible. Like almost everything else on this world, it was trapped in by the atmosphere, the impersonal and prejudiceless border guard of humanity. And he felt it pressing down on him more and more, each passing second.

5

THE PARAMEDICS loomed over him, their hands wandering over his chest, checking his pulse. Feeling sensation entering back into his limbs, filling his muscles, Stanley coughed and, despite the paramedic attempting to keep him lying down, he sat up straight.

Several concerned faces stared down on him.

He rubbed his temples and then his eyeballs.

"Are you okay?" Nick said, from among the crowd.

Stanley nodded and tried to get up.

One of the paramedics reached out and held his shoulder. "Madam? Please don't make any sudden movements. We just want to do a few more examinations, see that you're all right."

Madam?

Stanley gazed down at his chest where a pair of compact, rounded breasts stuck out. He brushed his hand against them, feeling a shudder pass through him. He stared at his trousers, knowing what he would find down there when he got them off.

When the paramedics had finished their examinations, Nick and Alan helped Stanley to his feet and then back over to his work station. The way they held him, their light touch, like he were a delicate flower, felt strange and alien. He perched on the edge of his chair, watching as the colours blurred back into one another, creating whole figures once more. Everything turned lucid, sharpened.

Nick gave him a couple of pats on the shoulder, then told him to come and see him if he had any problems at all.

When Stanley spoke to reply, his pitch was high and floaty. The voice was foreign to him but he had no doubt that it had shaken his own vocal cords.

Alan glanced around the office and then crouched down at Stanley's side. "You gave us all a scare there. Thought you might be having a stroke or something."

"Yeah," Stanley said.

And then Alan reached out and squeezed Stanley's knee. "Talk about it tonight, okay?"

Stanley's whole body trembled and his blood pumped to his chest. He stared into Alan's eyes, losing himself in them. He pressed his back into his chair, trying to escape Alan's clutches.

With a smile Alan rose and then paced round the cubicle to his own workstation, shooting Stanley another few glances.

Stanley steadied himself at his desk. He looked over the pictures. The ones of him and Mary had disappeared, now all that remained were pictures of himself and Alan. They were in various places: by a lake, in a London cab, drinking together in a pub. He leant closer.

Stanley inspected his own face in those photos. There was no mistaking that it was him in the photos, but he was also, without a doubt, female. He supposed that if he had had a sister she might well have looked similar to him in those photographs.

As he looked up he caught Alan's eye, peering over the cubicle. When he reached to the back of the chair, for his coat, he found his thick overcoat to be gone, replaced by a flimsy light-purple jacket.

He got up and stumbled back, falling onto another desk.

Alan immediately leapt up from his workstation and ran to Stanley's side. He reached out to support him, eyes wild with concern. "Still feeling faint, aren't you? Think it'd be a good idea to get you back home."

Stanley kept his eyes glued to the photographs stuck around his computer monitor and tried to envision what kind of life he had with Alan, whether he was happy or bored, contented or frustrated.

After helping Stanley back into his seat, Alan headed off to Nick's office, to ask permission to take Stanley home.

Stanley watched Alan return across the office floor, with a slight smile on his lips.

"Okay," Alan said. "I'm going to take you back."

A numbness draped over Stanley's muscles and bones, locking them into place. He could do nothing to run or escape from this demented dimension, so he just went along with it.

Alan helped Stanley into his coat and then past the several sets of eyes watching them go, mouthing well-wishes as they went.

Nick emerged from his office and wished Stanley a speedy recovery.

Stanley didn't respond, however, he was too occupied on his own thoughts and how this was all really happening. When he got out into the reception area he looked over to Jenny, busy chatting away on the phone.

She caught Stanley's eye and put the phone down. "Heard about what happened." She pranced out from behind the reception desk and gripped Stanley's hands in hers.

The feel of her smooth skin was different for Stanley, as a woman. He had none of the pitted urges he had felt as a man, and he savoured her concerned glow, tickling his tear ducts. Before he cried, he turned away from her, back into Alan's waiting arms.

Jenny called after them. "Take it easy, okay. Watch some films, drink some soup. Soon you'll be better, I'm sure."

They took a taxi back to the house. Alan took mercy on Stanley, not pressing him into conversation. Although he had never experienced it himself, Stanley recognised the easy silence between them—that of an old married couple.

They passed through several neighbourhoods on the edge of

town and Stanley grew anxious. He knew the route to his house like the back of his hand, and they were going in precisely the opposite direction. But then he recalled his previous episode, when he had returned home to find someone else living there. He felt his pocket for the key. It was still there, and he was sure it would open his house door—his real house.

The taxi kept on droning along.

They pulled up outside the house. It was a three or four bedroom, detached, with a garage and a large gravel driveway. The exterior had been plastered with shingle and rocks. Alan paid the driver and they got out. Alan rested his hand in the small of Stanley's back, sending a chill up his spine.

The inside of the house was well-kept and clean. Stanley noticed the coat rack at the door and, what he presumed to be, his coats hanging there. Beneath it there were several boots and shoes, which he also thought to be his. At least he had inherited a larger wardrobe.

Alan said, "You just tuck yourself up on the sofa, love."

Stanley suffered a kiss on the cheek and then went through into what turned out to be the sitting room. He tested the sofa. It dipped under his weight, stuffed with feathers. He set himself down on the pillows, his head throbbing and the area around his eyes feeling puffy and sore. He had to get the hell out this . . . whatever *this* was.

Alan brought in a pair of steaming cups of tea on a wooden tray. Some of the tea had spilt into little brown puddles.

For the first time, Stanley understood the childish, hopeless streak in men. He accepted one of the cups and blew on it.

"How're you feeling?" Alan said, eyebrows knitted.

"Fine."

"Don't think we should go to the hospital?"

Stanley shrugged and then slurped more tea.

"Okay then," Alan said, with a sigh. "I'd better get on with some of my emails. Don't want them to be piled up when I get in tomorrow morning. Shout if you need anything." He got up, leaving Stanley alone.

Stanley got his head back together and then rose from the sofa. He walked around the house, taking in the various rooms, before reaching the master bedroom. He entered and looked it over. He wondered which side of the bed was his.

On one of the bedside tables he spotted a remote control, for the television which hung on the opposite wall, on the other were a pile of books. He supposed the book side was his, or his female self's. Feeling a huge weight pressing down on him, like the clouds might descend to crush his brain, he slipped beneath the covers, of what he thought to be his side of the bed, and he felt himself fall away into sleep.

Stanley woke when he felt the bed tremble. He stirred slightly but didn't crane his neck or open his eyes to see. He knew it was Alan. It must be night by now.

Alan's arm reached out and brushed the back of his neck.

A tingle ran through Stanley's bones, right through his stomach. He curled himself tighter into a ball and squeezed his eyes shut.

Alan kissed his shoulder and then his upper arm. "You better now?"

Stanley shuddered.

"Had a good sleep?"

Stanley opened one eye and peered out at Alan, who had spooned his body around his. He wanted to hunch back, to knock him away, and to run out of the house. But what would it mean? He would just end up back where he had started before.

The other option was to lie there in bed and let Alan have his way with him. The idea was repulsive to Stanley. He had known

Alan for so long, twenty years or more, ever since he had started working at the company, and any sense of sexiness which might have once existed had been ground away over years of familiarity.

He flinched at another of Alan's touches.

Alan pulled away. "What? What is it?" He let loose a long and drawn out sigh. "Is something the matter?"

"No," Stanley said, a tear running down his cheek.

"Sorry, it's just . . . I thought that—"

"Don't worry."

Alan slunk back further in the bed, more distant. "Okay."

Stanley prised off the bed cover and stepped out, the thick carpet tickling in between his toes. He headed for the door.

"What is it, love?" Alan said. "I can get it for you if you like."

"No," Stanley said, pausing at the opening, looking out into the gloomy landing.

Alan turned over on his side, his back to Stanley. "All right."

Stanley crept along the landing. He paused to examine a photo on the wall of himself with Alan, standing on a ski slope. They each had a pair of skis over their shoulders, reddened cheeks and white smiles, snow-capped mountains sprawled out in the background.

Stanley had never, ever, in his life had the urge to go skiing. This might be Alan's life but it certainly wasn't his. He thought of the power which Alan had taken to mould him to his interests, get him to be like him. So what if Stanley's life hadn't worked out to be a utopia, at least he had been getting along perfectly fine, not hurting anybody, being anonymous? And yet, he had the distinct feeling he had missed out, on the basics, the family things. But he would have none of that with Alan.

He stepped into the bathroom, drew the door shut behind him and slipped on the bolt lock. He set the upturned toilet seat down and sat on it, thinking. He glanced upward at the medicine cabinet, a mirror.

He thought he looked truly ridiculous as a woman. It would all be over soon. But he knew that he couldn't put up with it for a second longer. He got up and flipped open the medicine cabinet. From within he dug out a couple of packets of painkillers. He inspected the contents: one full packet, the other nearly full.

He cracked the pills out of their packets, into the palm of his hand, and then he brought them up to his mouth and knocked them back without water. His gooey saliva helped them down his throat, to his stomach. And soon, once again, the whole world was spinning before his eyes.

6

ONCE MORE, Stanley found himself back where he had started. He remained static as the paramedics checked him over and, inevitably, finding nothing wrong, they cautiously helped him to his feet, back to his desk.

Stanley had returned to his former body and the photographs around his computer screen had all disappeared. There was nothing except empty space. Just like it was back in his real life. He wondered whether he had finally returned.

When Alan peered over the top of the cubicle, his face still sketched with concern, Stanley gave him a sliver of a smile, reassuring his workmate and allowing him to return to his day job. He did the same.

The working day finished and gradually the office emptied of functionaries. Stanley remained at his computer, staring at the ever-growing list of emails, clicking, scanning, replying and repeating. He hardly acknowledged Alan when he bid Stanley a good evening, knowing that in a matter of hours all this would change, and he would return to the same starting position, as always. Soon Stanley was the only employee remaining.

Vacuum cleaners hummed into life and the cleaning ladies chattered away. One of them, with a grey-stained, blue pinstriped apron appeared at his cubicle. On noticing him there she startled and apologised, saying that she'd thought everyone had gone home for the evening.

Stanley kept his eyes glued to the screen, checking the time in the bottom corner every couple of minutes as it ticked closer to midnight. Only a few hours left. If he decided to go home now, to try and open up and go inside, he had no way of knowing what might greet him. He could go out, in the street, of course, while away the time down there, but what use would it serve? He was stuck in an infinite loop. Whatever he did now would have no impact whatsoever in a matter of hours.

A more senior-looking cleaner with blue-tainted hair and thick black eyeliner approached Stanley at his desk. She clung to a vacuum cleaner. "Come on, then, sir. You've got to clear out. We need to tidy up."

Stanley met her gaze slowly. He felt bags weighing on his eyes, pulling them down his face. He just stared back at her, with his lips pressed tight together.

"Well?" she said.

Stanley returned to his computer screen, back to his work.

"Look, mister, don't think that just because you're wearing a suit you can do whatever you want. You've done your job now it's our turn, all right? My girls need to clear up this space and they can't do that with you sitting there."

Stanley stayed silent.

She rounded him and located herself between Stanley and his computer monitor. "You speak English?"

Stanley looked past her body, at the luminescent screen.

"Oi!"

Reluctantly he turned his attention back to her.

"You are all to be out of here by seven. Do you know why?"

Stanley kept his head still.

"If we clean up here and then tomorrow your boss comes in to find a mess somewhere we're the ones that'll get in trouble. How do you like that? At this rate we won't be out of here till midnight."

Although Stanley sympathised with the woman, understood and empathised with her situation, he had no intention of stepping out into that fierce and unfamiliar world. There was simply no point. And he was convinced that his resolve outweighed the cleaning woman's.

She grabbed hold of the back of his chair and shook it. "Out!"

He curled his fingers around the edge of the seat, clamping himself in place.

After about half a minute of shaking the woman gave up, sighed and then, with the rustle of bin liner, she continued at her work, emptying the bins, while the other women polished and mopped.

Around eight o'clock the woman approached him once more. "Well, I hope that you're happy." She shook her head. "When your boss gets in tomorrow morning and sees the state of your workspace there'll be hell to pay, let me tell you." She snorted, then called, "Val! Hazel! Get your coats!"

The other two women emerged, one bearing a dust cloth and the other a bucket and mop. With the senior woman in the lead, they headed out of the office. Their shoes clacked down the stairs and out of earshot.

Stanley opened another email.

An hour or so later Stanley felt overwhelming hunger pangs, but he repressed them. There was no point. They would disappear of their own accord soon enough.

As he scanned through another sequence of meaningless, pointless emails he marvelled at his situation and the nature of eternity—that was what he was living, wasn't it? If this were some kind of afterlife or dead end in the nature of time and the universe then he wanted to get off. He was ready for the big sleep if it came knocking.

He decided that staying in the same place was just what he needed to do. Perhaps the only reason he had been cursed to live out the same reality several times over was because of his wanting to explore, go elsewhere. As he thought more and more about it he became more and more resolved to the fact that he had to stay just here, right in this spot where he had suffered his episode, in the hope that he might reverse the effects.

The door to the office squeaked open once more and the regular, dampened *thud* of boots sounded on the thin, hard carpet. A portly security guard with his baseball cap pivoted back on his head smiled at him over the cubicle. "Working late, sir?"

Stanley gave him a brief glance then returned to his computer screen.

The guard coughed. "Big project, is it?"

"Something like that."

"Ah, right."

"Is there a problem?" Stanley said.

The guard scratched his flaky forehead and frowned. "It's just that I have to lock up the building." He smiled again. "You know how it is. So . . . do you think you could finish up with whatever you're doing?"

"Lock me up with it, thanks."

The guard's smile faltered. "Can't do that, I'm afraid, sir. Against company policy. Health and Safety."

"It's okay," Stanley said, turning his attention to his computer screen.

"Erm," the guard said, playing with his cap, adjusting the peak. "Do you have a car? If you like I could call you a taxi."

Stanley didn't respond.

The guard broke out in another smile. "Sure you've got your wife . . . kids waiting?"

"Nope."

"Ah, right."

Stanley busied himself with a reply to an email he had overlooked for several weeks. He started off with an apology and then fulfilled the request. Although he knew this all to be in vain he hoped to throw off the guard, to make the guard back down to his request. The guard would have to call the police if he wanted him out of the building.

The guard jingled his keys. "Really, sir, I have to ask you to leave."

"I can't do that, I'm sorry."

"I . . . I, well, then I'll need to call my superior."

"Okay."

The guard lingered over him, unmoving. "But I don't want to do that. He'll be at home with his family now. It would be much easier if you'd just agree to leave."

"I can't."

"Erm, but you have to," the guard said, then mumbled something else about company policy.

"You can just leave me here. Lock me up inside."

"But what if there's a fire?"

"It's okay."

The guard seemed to consider this eventuality a moment and then shook his head. "That wouldn't work at all." He took a step back. "I think I'll have to call my superior."

"Okay."

The guard stood on the periphery of the cubicle another few seconds before backing away completely and, with a large and drawn out sigh, trod out of the door, back down the stairs and—Stanley presumed—back to his position at the desk, with all the security camera monitors.

Stanley closed down his email and then powered off his computer. He had been serious when he had told the guard that he literally couldn't leave this place. It was like someone had installed a magnet in the seat of his trousers and he could no longer remove himself from this location. Time was ticking toward midnight, when he supposed he would return to his starting position.

Stanley slid back on his chair and glanced around the room.

He noticed a security camera hanging up in the corner, its tiny red light gleaming. He weaved through the work cubicles and got to the light switch positioned at the door which led down the stairs. He flipped it off and then dropped to his knees and crawled his way along the wall, keeping out of the camera's line of sight. He presumed that it had some kind of night vision functionality.

He returned to his desk, slipped his jacket off the back and then sleuthed his way through the maze of cubicles, finding one positioned near a window and huddled underneath the desk, drawing his overcoat around him like a blanket.

In the gloom he waited for a long time, hearing his breath loud in his ears. Being like this reminded him of when he had been a child and he had hidden from his parents. It gave him a youthful thrill knowing that the guard would re-enter the office at any moment. His heart thunked in his skull, sloshing his brain around. He must be close to returning.

Sure enough the security guard's footsteps slapped up the staircase and the office door swung open. "Sir?"

Stanley chewed on his lower lip as he held his breath.

The guard stepped inside, the soles of his shoes scuffing the rough carpet. "Sir?"

Stanley closed his eyes and drifted away into his own thoughts.

The guard continued his stroll into the office. There was a metallic *click*. Stanley presumed that he had turned on a torch. The guard's breath was husky and uneven. He drew closer and then halted—when he'd reached his work station, he presumed. The guard grunted and then his footsteps sounded on the carpet, heading back toward the office door.

Stanley listened in as the lock snapped shut and the guard's footsteps proceeded on their way.

Quite sure that the guard had disappeared for good, Stanley emerged from his hiding place. He stayed crouched, not trusting the security camera, and he located his own desk. As before he hunched beneath it and made himself comfortable with his overcoat. It made him think of a dog's bed.

Feeling his mind rattle and churn he laid his head down on the cool, rough carpet and shut his eyes, praying that he would wake up and everything would be back to normal tomorrow.

After several hours of tossing and turning he couldn't find sleep, so he got up and drank water from the taps in the toilets. The water flushed down his throat and gargled through his depleted system. It felt good, refreshing. He looked himself in the mirror, staring into his own black eyes and wondered, if he weren't himself, who he really was. Had Stanley Smith, his true identity, simply been lost in the world? Did his concept of himself really exist? Had it ever really existed?

With those, and several other questions, rolling around his brain, he found his way through the darkness back to his work station, curled himself into a ball and tucked his head into his chest, as if he were on a plane about to perform a crash landing.

7

THE WORDS ONLY reached Stanley as muffled, muted screams. He glowered at his screen, its irradiated light. His whole world burst at the seems. Molecules trickled in around the edges, whizzing past him, smashing into one another, tickling him all over.

And then it all retreated. The jagged frontiers returned. The world came into focus.

He lay on his back, staring up at the ceiling, picking out the little holes, the pinpricks in the plasterboard tiles. Words washed over him like waves sucking at pebbles on a beach, drawing his thoughts further and further away, down into the undertow.

He tried to move his arms but nothing happened.

Someone appeared above him, their mouth flapping wide, eyes bulging. It was Nick.

Stanley tried his hardest to understand but he had no way of understanding what Nick was communicating to him. It felt like someone had stuffed his ears with cloth.

Nick was shouting over him, telling someone something.

Jenny appeared in the periphery of Stanley's vision. She was frozen in panic, clearly not responding to Nick's commands.

Stanley closed his eyes and listened to the intense silence filling his mind. When he attempted to open his eyes again he found he was unable. A clear and stomach-churning sensation of falling accompanied his descent downward into the eternal darkness. This was the end, he was sure of it.

A single *blip* filled his hearing, like a beacon in the middle of a still ocean, nothing all round, just water lapping at its base.

Stanley stirred from his sleep. He crooked open and eye and took in his surroundings. The walls were washed in white, his bedspread was white and there was a tube sticking out of his arm. He was in a hospital.

A figure blurred through the air, drawing closer to him.

He squinted to make out their form.

It was a doctor. He wore a stethoscope coiled round his neck and had a square jaw. While he spoke he kept his hands collected neatly behind his back. The words shifted in and out, passing through Stanley's consciousness. "Stanley?" the doctor said.

Stanley groaned in reply.

A smile tweaked the corner of the doctor's mouth. "I see . . . recuperating . . . procedure."

When Stanley attempted to say 'yes' his vocal cords completely deserted him. All he could do was moan.

"Don't . . . it's important you . . ."

The sinking feeling returned to Stanley's body, as if his brain were melting through his skull, down into his spine and out of his buttocks. The doctors words faded totally and the darkness, the silence, resumed.

He awoke in the dark. Not the dark of his mind. He could make out the crispness of the physical gloom, subtly different. He made out forms. A cabinet across the room. The multi-coloured lights on the machine burbling along beside him. There was a clock with a neon red display attached to the wall opposite. Now it read eleven fifty-seven.

He could think again. Thoughts cranked their way through his brain one-by-one, all asking the same question: Where am I going next?

In the matter of another few blinks, the clock flickered over to midnight.

0.00

He waited for the familiar spinning, to return to work. But nothing at all happened. He just lay there.

The clock flashed over to one minute past midnight, and Stanley knew that somehow he had escaped the infinite loop. Was this where his destiny wished for him to end up?

Tentative, he attempted to raise his left arm. He could lift it a matter of millimetres, a quantity which he presumed to be indistinguishable to anyone but himself. But it was progress, he was sure of it. He was back on a fixed plain of reality.

But which one?

The machine beside him hummed to itself and he watched a tangerine liquid flow through the tube and into his vein. He was certain he felt it bubble round his blood stream, penetrate his blood vessels and enter his system. His head felt light and his eyes drooped. Sleep was draping itself back over him once more.

When he awoke dawn was breaking. Fresh rays of sunlight penetrated his metallic blinds. One of the rays caught his eye, sending a flash of pain through him. But Stanley didn't mind. This was his world now. No one could tear it away from him, even if they tried.

As he absorbed the room, he noticed a man seated in a chair, facing away from him, looking out through the window. A small circular bald patch poked through his grey hair. As if he could feel Stanley's gaze fall on him, the man said, "You're awake."

Stanley summoned saliva and swallowed it back, moistening his throat enough to respond. ". . . Yes."

The next question forming on Stanley's tongue was who this man was. But, before he could string the words together, the man tilted his head to the side, so that Stanley got him in profile. A faint note of familiarity stuck him. He had seen this man before. When this had all started, at the bus stop. The man he had bumped into.

The man rose from the chair and faced Stanley. He smiled warmly. "Yes, you remember me, don't you? Back when all this started."

"How . . . how do you—"

"How do I know?" He chuckled. "Good question. Just what I would ask if our situation were reversed. You broke the system, Stan. Great job. Only took you a few goes. Fast leaner."

Stanley lay on the bed, each breath a struggle. Although he manifested patience, he was hungry for answers. He sucked in air, to tell the man to hurry up.

The man strode forward. "Please, Stanley, don't waste your efforts. You've been through a lot, you need to recuperate. Just lie there and listen to me."

Reluctant, Stanley loosened his muscles and watched the man, like a toddler immobilised in a high-chair, waiting for its parent to bring it nourishment.

"What you've seen are a collection of possibilities, ways that you might've lived, or that you might live in the future."

Through his numb body, his aching limbs and wheeling mind, he managed a slight smile. "What is . . . this? A . . . Chris . . . Christ . . . mas Carol?"

The man chortled. "You have a nice sense of humour, Stanley. I knew you deserved a chance."

"A . . . chance?"

All of a sudden, the man lurched forward and seized hold of the tube feeding Stanley.

He gasped, feeling the liquid cease to flow into him. An aching pain ratcheted up through him, spiralling through his chest, through his neck, before settling in his brain.

"No more questions," the man said, his mouth a slit.

Stanley relaxed himself, fixed his stare on the man's nimble fingers, shutting off his pain relief. He resisted the urge to tell the man to let go of the tube, knowing that would only exacerbate the situation.

The man cocked his head. "We understand each other?" he said, loosening his grip on the tube, then letting go completely.

Stanley relished the painkillers seeping back into his system.

"That's it, good boy. No more questions."

Stanley's head lolled on his neck and he felt like he was floating, upward to the ceiling.

The man took a step back and crossed his arms over his chest. "So, it's decision time, Stanley. Which reality is it going to be? Which of those would make you the happiest?"

Not knowing he should speak, not wanting the wonderful woozy feeling to end, he stayed silent.

"You can talk for this part."

Stanley sucked up all the air, thinking back over his life, his original life. He had lived alone in that large house, he'd had the steady job, he'd been happy—hadn't he? That day he had been running late to work, it had meant everything to him, getting there on time. But what had been the importance of it? Had anyone even noticed? Over and over he told himself he was valued, that without that reality—his reality—he would be missed.

"Tricky, is it?" the man said, cocking an eyebrow. "Thought you had more about you, Stan. Going to have to rush you, haven't got all day. Doctor will be in here before long. What's it going to be?"

There was only one choice he could make. He knew it himself. What he had missed all along, what he had been missing out for his entire life. There was only one way to etch his image on the world—really put something back.

The man's face firmed up. He puffed up his cheeks. "Come on, Stan!"

Through the near-paralysis, Stanley felt his throat throbbing with the weight of the words.

The man cupped his hand round his ear. "Can't hardly hear you." He drew closer and bent over. "Give it some welly, eh?"

Every time Stanley took a breath it felt like the air had been ripped from his mouth, gone before he had a chance to use it. But he hunched himself back on the bed, stabbed his tongue downward and said, "The family. I choose the family."

The man sighed then examined his fingernails. "So predictable. So, so predictable." He shook his head. "You can't imagine how old this gets after a few goes, really, it's ridiculous." He gripped the labels of his tweed jacket and jerked it straight over his shoulders. "None of the guys ever go for the woman option, don't tell me you aren't curious?"

Stanley stayed quiet, worried that this man might turn his decision round if he uttered a word.

"Not talking, eh? Don't blame you. You've made your choice, you want to stick by it. Nice. Solid. I can see you're going to be an outstanding father."

Stanley's eyeballs rolled in their sockets as he followed the man over to the door.

The man lingered a moment, glanced back at Stanley then shot him a wide, toothy grin. He slipped out the door and Stanley could relax.

Stanley lay where he was, watching the sun come up, through the blinds and flood the room.

When a nurse came in she used her hand to shield the light from her eyes. "Blooming heck, it's a bit bright in here, isn't it?"

Stanley murmured something.

The nurse adjusted the blinds, bringing them shut a notch.

"No," Stanley said.

The nurse flinched, then looked over at him. She pursed her lips. "Oh, Mr Smith, you're awake."

"Leave . . . please leave the blinds."

The nurse paused a moment then smiled and did as he said, unravelling the blinds, returning to them to their almost open position. She checked his machine and then left him alone again.

Throughout the rest of the day, Stanley remained where he was as various medical personnel buzzed round him, checking his vital signs, looking over his complexion and speaking to him—although he never responded.

Later on, he heard familiar voices in the corridor and knew that this was real—this was his reality now whatever had been before. He tilted his head to the door and watched as his two children rushed in, leapt onto his bed, threw their tiny arms round him.

Tears welled in his eyes. A profound warmth grasped him.

Then Mary appeared in the doorway. She hung back at first, a neutral expression set in her lips. Then, as if prodded from behind by some off-stage hand, she grinned at him and joined his children in embracing him.

This would be the happiest memory of Stanley's life, if only he were to die right here.

COLONY C

THE WAVES OF WARMTH coming from the open-plan, chrome-surfaced restaurant kitchens scalded Bettie's skin. She was sure that—when she woke up tomorrow morning—she would have come out in a horrific heat rash. She was always coming out in rashes of some sort or other, and there wasn't enough concealer in her specific flesh tone in the whole of Martian Colony C to sort it out.

She looked about the restaurant. She had come underdressed. As *usual*. Just look at them: the men all dressed in smart suits and ties, the women in cleavage-inducing cocktail dresses. And here *she* was in this frumpy, unironed, lilac-coloured blouse *thing* over this decade-old pair of washed-out black jeans.

Just fetch any old thing out of the back of the wardrobe, that was what her daughter, Millie, had told her. *It isn't a fancy place.*

Bettie sniffed the air.

Fish.

Goodness.

Yes, really.

She examined the circular tables—with their white tablecloths —where the other diners sat. Saw them tucking into their dinners. Their *shellfish* dinners. Why, just thinking about it, about those gooey, fleshy *fish-stinking* insides on those otherwise spotless, white porcelain plates was enough to bring the bile frothing up her throat, and stinging the back of her tongue.

A *fish* restaurant.

So, it was true, her daughter really had *no clue* who she really was.

That Bettie—only her *mother*—was *allergic* to fish.

Had been all these forty long years of her life.

Bettie dipped her hand into the pocket of her jeans. Withdrew a well-snotted tissue, and held it up to cover her nose and mouth. Shut her eyes. Tried to breathe normally. The clinking of cutlery on porcelain sounded like a dozen hammers clattering against a steel sheet.

She breathed deep.

Calm. Time to be calm now.

Calm? Time . . .

"Bettie?"

She opened her eyes, though she didn't need to.

She knew just who it was.

George.

Her *ex*-husband.

She felt her heart leap up to her throat. Hammer away at her tonsils.

No, no, no . . . this couldn't be happening. Not really. Not *really* happening.

All of a sudden she found herself breathing in his musky scent —that smell she'd lived with for eleven glorious years . . . ten of those marriage. The scent she'd woken to every morning. The scent she'd still smelled on the empty silk sheets of their bed for weeks after he had finally left for good. The way that he'd walked out of her life without realising just how deep a crater he was leaving in his wake.

"Is something the matter?" George asked.

Bettie managed to pin on a smile—that smile of hers she often brought out on polite occasions, a smile that she could use on just about anyone from security officers to elderly neighbours. And she used it now. She tried to put those sickly stenches to one side and then said, "Oh, no. Nothing's the matter—not at *all*." She blinked a couple of times and then summoned up the courage to look him over.

As always he looked well groomed, his hair swept into a side parting—still thick, though it was now a silver grey, rather than the jet-black it had once been. He still looked like a star from those films from the fifties that they used to so enjoy watching together. That was before she even got started on his lush, olive skin. He wore a charcoal suit with matching tie, all held together by a crisp, white shirt underneath. On his arm he had a younger —*much* younger—blond woman with reddish-brown hair and one of those laser-white smiles, which she was currently aiming at Bettie.

George seemed to remember himself. He broke off his gaze with Bettie and then held out his hand to introduce the blond woman. "This is Hurly," he said.

Bettie received Hurly's dainty, birdlike little hand and gave it a shake. She did a bit more smiling too. That same *polite* smile of hers. "Nice to meet you."

The handshaking done, George arched his shoulders, looked about the dining room, and then let loose a vague sigh. "Meeting up with anyone special tonight?"

Bettie felt her stomach knot . . . but, again, not because of the fish.

Why hadn't she told him? How had she thought that she could avoid him here what with there only being—*what?*—ten, fifteen thousand people on Mars?

She decided that now certainly *wasn't* the time and she kept up that same polite smile—willing him and his blond 'friend' away to their table; to go and suck fish guts.

"Uh, no," Bettie said. "Just an old friend, that's all."

George smiled a little wider, and she watched as the blond woman wrapped her fingers about his forearm and gave it a little squeeze—one of those subtle signals that she wanted to get away as soon as possible.

Bettie felt a dip of pleasure in her gut that she'd managed to have an effect on the girl—made her feel intimidated.

"Who?" George asked.

"Oh, no one you know," she said, taking on a lighter tone, and at the same time wondering if she'd overdone it.

After all, she still had feelings for George. She didn't *want* him to think that she was brushing him off, that she no longer cared for him, wouldn't ever accept him back into her life. Because he was a wonderful person—the greatest person she'd ever met.

. . . Well, the greatest *man* in any case.

But she had no choice. She had made her decisions, and now she had to go with them no matter how hard it was to cover her tracks.

He gave her an understanding smile, a slight nod. He looked about the restaurant again, spotting the bow-tied, waist-coated waiter creeping up on them. As the waiter stood by, waiting politely for them to finish up their conversation, George turned to Bettie and then, apparently on impulse, leaned forward and planted a gentle kiss on her cheek.

Bettie felt just about all the blood in her body rushing to her head. But she tried to pass it off with a slightly girlish giggle.

"It was nice to see you," George said, and then ventured off with the waiter pattering before them to a table over by the window, looking out onto the Martian plains, with a plastic *Reserved* sign propped up there.

Bettie watched the two of them take their seats—watched them sit down opposite each other, neither one breaking eye contact.

Love?

Was that it?

Were they in love?

Was *George* in love again?

She couldn't blame him—*how could she?*—after what she'd done to him.

After all the lies she'd told.

At the door, she saw her daughter. She broke off her thoughts, making her way over. Now they would have some serious words—imagine her daughter inviting her not only to a *fish* restaurant but to one which her ex-husband apparently frequented.

. . . .Then again, how was Millie to know?

———

"Really, Mum," Millie said. "We can go somewhere else if it's a problem."

"No, no," Bettie said as she sat down on the chair the waiter had pulled back for her. "These are good seats if nothing else." She realised that where Millie had reserved their table just happened to be three or four over from where George and his blond bombshell sat sucking at their oysters. Just like George, they had a view out over the Martian plains—lit up with simple fluorescent white lights, showing off all the bumps and rocks scattered about outside the bubble which protected the colony. She turned her attention back to her daughter Millie, sitting opposite.

Tonight she looked lovely, what with her long, sleek black hair unfurled down onto her exposed olive-skinned shoulder. She was wearing a mauve cocktail dress. Bettie knew she *never* would've been able to pull off a colour like it. She was just too red skinned to wear a tone like that, but on Millie it seemed to work just perfectly.

Millie's hazel eyes drifted over onto hers, and Bettie caught a whiff of her blueberry-inflected scent. It carried over the fishy smells of the restaurant, giving Bettie just a little respite.

Bettie had asked to see the vegetarian menu in the hope that there might be something which hadn't lived its life in a salt-water tank—she'd managed to find herself a Caesar salad which would do the trick . . . if not for her appetite, then for her figure.

Now that they each had a glass of white wine before them, Bettie found herself cooling down with each sip of alcohol. It was as if the stuff massaged her from the inside—as if it turned her guts gooey and made everything good again. But she had to be careful thinking like that. She couldn't forget what her therapist had told her about making sure *not* to use alcohol as a 'crutch' . . . as she had used it when George had left. No, she certainly couldn't go down *that* road again.

"Mum?" Millie said, her voice raised with girlish intonation—that intonation which Bettie recognised from Millie's nine-year-old self, usually attached to the word, 'Why?'

Bettie took a sip from her wine glass, and turned her attention back to her daughter. "Hmm?"

"Why do you keep looking over at that man and woman?"

Bettie felt her heart skip a beat. "What do you mean?"

Millie—her cheeks now with just a slight flush from the wine—leaned over the white tablecloth, taking care to rest her elbow just to one side of the silver cutlery. When she spoke, she dropped her voice to a conspiratorial whisper. "Well, I've noticed that every time I look up you're glancing over there—if I'm boring you then I can leave you to it, if you like."

For some reason this rubbed Bettie up the wrong way. She felt her heart beat harder. "Leave me?" she said. "Why? Why *would* you?"

Millie rolled her eyes and leaned back in her chair. She grasped her wine glass by the stem and knocked back the contents in a single gulp. She reached out for the gently perspiring bottle of wine and poured herself out another glass.

Sometimes Bettie wondered if Millie had got her wine genes.

"Relax," Millie said, clutching her fresh glass of wine to her breast. "I was just joking." She nodded over Bettie's shoulder then said, "But, seriously, what is it with that man? Is he someone you're interested in? Is there something I should know?"

Bettie met Millie's gaze—looked off over her shoulder again in the direction of George and his companion. She knew she would never get a better opportunity.

It was now or never, why should she keep playing this silly game?

So, taking a swig of her wine for just a touch of Dutch courage, Bettie delivered the hammer blow that she'd put off for so many years—that she'd covered up for so long with vague explanations and wishy-washy reasoning.

"That man," Bettie said, "is your father."

———

Bettie could have sworn, looking back on the occasion in her mind's eye, that at that particular moment the entire restaurant slipped into complete and total silence. In reality, though, she knew that—most likely—everything about them continued to grind about life as usual: that couples laughed to themselves, popped fish guts into their mouths or snuck pecked kisses across the table.

Bettie held still as she viewed her daughter in the flickering candlelight. In the fiery glow that sprung up between them. She watched as Millie's chest rose and fell as she attempted to wrestle with what she had just told her. She traced those beautiful hazel eyes . . . her *father's* eyes . . . bob about their sockets trying to get a hold on this information.

"But . . . but," Millie began but couldn't quite see her way to finishing.

Bettie decided that it was time to fill in a little more information. "Me and your father, we were *married* for ten years."

"I . . . you," Millie said, her eyes appearing to almost bulge from their sockets now, and her bottom lip wobbling as if on the brink of losing control. "You told me that I was . . . I was from a . . . a *bank.*"

Bettie gave a solemn nod and then shifted her attention to her wine glass stem—to where she was smoothing her fingertips up and down the veneer of the glass. She really had opened the Big Box of Tricks here, and she couldn't simply go a little way, she had to explain it all. Was it simply having seen George again—*having run into him*—that had brought all of this bubbling back to the surface; that had sent her on a fatal guilt trip which had ended in her giving away her greatest secret? Because, one thing was for certain, there was no taking it back now.

She waited out the few seconds for Millie to get control of herself. She knew she couldn't just blurt all this out at once. She needed to give her daughter enough time to digest. But, at the same time, she felt a weight on her chest, and she knew that she strived to rid herself of this burden.

She started slow.

"It's right that I told you that you were from a bank—that I had the artificial insemination done."

'Artificial', she had always hated that word, always thought that it suggested that there was something *fake* about the process— what, because there was no 'love making' involved, was that the thing about it? It was funny that once she'd told that very first lie, told the very first person that Millie had been the result of a sperm bank, there had been no turning back. She had found herself shifted into that group of women deemed too 'unattractive' to find a man on one of the three Martian colonies. And so—above all else —she supposed that she had lived out her life as one of those artificial-insemination mothers. Had lived with the stigma. With those unflattering comments, all of them, without exception, made behind her back. The truth of it was that—however she had lived her life—she *wasn't* one of those women at all.

No, she had found a man, and he had got her pregnant.

And then he had left.

And she had never . . . how to put it . . . *got around* to telling him.

She eyed Millie over the rim of her wine glass, and the glow from the candle between them. She saw that Millie's eyes had a pinkish tone to them and that she was very likely close to tears. There was nothing she could do about that. Now that she had begun to tell the truth it would be an intently painful process. And there was no telling if Millie would forgive her at all.

"But . . . why, Mum. I . . . I don't understand why you lied to me through all these years."

This was a question that Bettie simply had no answer for. And so she chose to say nothing at all. She could explain later on if she *truly* cared to hear her out. But otherwise it was best to leave Millie only the biggest pieces to swallow for the time being.

She reached across the table for Millie's hand, slipped her fingers over her daughter's, and wrestled her gaze onto her own. "Look. I don't want you to think that I don't love you—that I haven't loved you enough to tell you the truth, but it's just that, the way things were, it was the best way to leave it."

"But *why*?" Millie said, her voice cracking about the edges for the first time.

"Your father," Bettie said, "he . . . he and I . . . we'd . . ." but Bettie just didn't seem able to finish—her voice simply lost its strength to go on.

"What?"

"We *tried* for so long—we wanted a child of our own for such a long time, and your father . . . he, ah, he . . . he *couldn't* . . . I mean, he *didn't* have the, uh, . . ."

"What? What, Mum, just *tell* me."

"He was impotent, that was what the doctors said. They said that he would never be able to have a child of his own. And . . . and your father told me, told me that if we couldn't have a child together then it was better . . . better for *both* of us, if he left."

"And you *let* him?"

Bettie nodded, already seeing the glint of the candlelight off the surface of her wine and longing to take another sip. She knew the wine would act as an elixir, that it would unfog her mind —*sharpen* her thoughts. She resisted.

"But . . . but," Millie started again, "if you got *pregnant* and with *his* child then why didn't you go to him—why didn't you *go back* to him?"

Bettie shook her head lightly and then gazed on out through the window—out across the Martian plains, all stretched out there, all floodlit and desolate. "It was too late, dear. It was *far* too late."

"*Why?*" Millie said, this time with genuine malice in her voice —a real cutting edge to the word.

"He . . . he had gone. Your father, he was serving on recon, and he took the first mission, a *five-year* mission off away from the planet, to do . . . I don't know . . . *something* . . . something else."

"So? Why didn't you tell him then?"

"Five years—it's a long time. A long time here, on Colony C, doing nothing but raising a child, you must understand that. I had already . . . become *accustomed* to it, to all that went with it, to being a single mother, to being an *artificially inseminated* mother."

A single tear rolled down Millie's left cheek. It stopped when it reached the base of her chin, rested a moment, and then plopped down onto the white table cloth leaving a damp mark thick with eyeliner. "I . . . I can't believe this."

Bettie nodded along. "I know, dear, it's a *lot* to take in. I'm so sorry."

Millie's gaze hardened and her expression turned from one of upset to one of pure, unchecked anger. She glowered at Bettie over the rim of her wine glass. "I mean, I can't believe that you, all this time, hid this information from me because you wanted to save *your* reputation, that you didn't think to tell your *own* daughter that she wasn't cooked up in a test tube after all." She drew a quivering breath, and, for a moment, Bettie was certain that she was going to pass out. But she stayed solid in her seat, and continued. "Do you realise what *I* went through? With all the kids at school *knowing* just where I came from? Do you *know* what kids at school called kids like me? Huh? Do you?"

Bettie thought she could hazard a guess. She knew that Millie had to vent her emotions—that it was important that she vent her emotions.

"*You*," Millie said, her gaze now carrying a real fire. "You're a *liar*."

Though Bettie had admitted as much to herself a long while ago it was very different to hear that word directed at her—actually spoken by another person. But it *was* the truth. And there was no getting around it.

With a flurry of limbs, Millie shoved herself up from the table and stalked off in the direction of the toilets.

———

Bettie didn't look around to watch her go. She just stared at the rim of her glass for a moment and then, feeling that twinge at the base of her gut, reached out for it. She pressed the glass up against her lips and then drank long and hard till all she could smell, all she could taste, was the white wine, the alcohol steaming up through her, and sending her blood bubbling.

She looked on out to the Martian plains, thinking about all that time she'd waited. Every one of those five years she'd spent with Millie. How she'd thought no less than a thousand times about how she would tell George. And how—each time she prepared herself to do so—she realised she simply couldn't. The web of lies that she'd woven about her and her daughter's life was simply too complex. Too *thick* to be broken with a single swipe.

He had had his life—had made peace with the fact that he would never had children.

He had made *his* plans just as she'd made her own.

And when he'd returned from that mission of his she saw how confidently he walked. How he had set himself up within the structure of the colony—observed the women that he bedded, and the times he had. She knew that it would do neither him or her any good to reveal that what the doctor had told him, all that time ago —that he would one hundred per cent *never* have children—was a falsehood. He had built his own life by then and it was well beyond Bettie's remit to bring that all crashing down. Especially when no children arrived from the other women he liaised with.

Bettie was only aware of the passing time when she reached the bottom of her wine glass.

She realised Millie wasn't coming back.

She reached behind her for the strap of her handbag—hanging off the back of her chair—and she drew it up onto her shoulder.

Before she rose, she glanced around, looked to the table where George and his companion sat. She was surprised to see Millie there, standing over them, holding her hands clutched at her waist.

From the looks of George's widened mouth, Millie had told him everything.

That was how it should be.

Everything would come crashing down now.

And there was nothing Bettie could do to control it.

In a single, swift motion, she rose to her feet, and without so much as looking over her shoulder another time, she padded her way gently off toward the door of the restaurant. As she slipped on out of the place she thought someone called out her name, though she couldn't be entirely sure. In any case, a few seconds later, she was encapsulated in a personal transport and humming off on her way back to her apartment.

If anyone needed her they knew just where to find her.

Where she'd always been.

CLEAN TEETH OF THE
DISPOSSESSED

T HE STENCH was the strangest thing about being here, on the Plains.

The way Imogen had imagined it, there would be a raw stench of rotting meat. So palpable as to send shimmers down her spine. But the smell, thinking about it a little more, was far more akin to leather. Just a sort of sleek, clean smell. That smell which confirmed that a hide had been divorced from its animal host; cured and preserved for time to come.

There was a certain time-eternal sense to the place.

As she slunk out of the shadows, she caught her twin brother —*Gut's*—eye.

Like her, he wore nothing more than a bunch of hastily sewn together rags, which, on account of their constant wearing, had taken on a muddy brown tone. Even in the darkness, with only the intermittent sheen from the faraway spotlights for illumination, she could make out those pale blue eyes of his, and the way they glinted softly. In the same way, she supposed, her own eyes glinted.

She planted her feet in a browned tuft of grass, feeling the soil underfoot soggy—*stodgy*—and she gazed out over the whole heap of bodies.

It really was horrific.

It was just as bad as they said back at Camp.

The way the bodies continued to wear their clothes, and how they clutched their hands—now reduced to only knobbly, mud-splattered bones—to their chests as if they still had something to protect. The bodies were maybe mounted four or five high. They had been thrown into their final resting places in any old position.

She sucked as her teeth—a nervous habit of hers—and tasted her own saliva.

The most unnerving thing, by far, was the silence.

Back at the Camp there was nothing but noise: chattering people, the stirrings of horses, and the constant flow of water, seemingly all around.

Out here, though, it was quiet.

Deathly quiet.

She glanced back over at Gut, and—without needing to utter so much as a word between them—they set about their search.

Looking for what might prove to be the key to their birth.

———

"Imma? Imma?"

Imogen poked her head up from where she was working at a particular corpse. As she'd searched through several of them, she'd been a little taken off guard when the bones had turned to dust beneath her touch. But, by now, she'd just about got used to it. Getting used to the older corpses—the ones which had already succumbed to the flames.

In the background, over their shoulders, she could make out the long cement wall of the Camp, and the searchlights which spun around and illuminated the faraway sky. Occasionally, one of the circles of light would swim out over the plains, lick its way along the earth, though its range would stop long before it neared Imogen and her brother.

She glanced over to Gut, who was about twenty paces away from her, checking over another body. "What?" she said, taking care to keep her voice hushed.

He left the body he was searching, and—head bowed as he picked his way through the corpses—he approached. When he drew up close, she saw he wore a faint smile. "You think it's weird how they all have perfect teeth?"

"What?"

He shrugged. "You know, like how going through them, looking in their mouths, how they don't seem to have had any of their teeth rot away—nothing like that."

"I hadn't thought about it," Imogen said, turning her attention back to the body which she now stood on. "I was a little more concerned about finding the ring."

This shut Gut up—a mirror image of herself, he dug about in the body which lay alongside.

Imogen thought back to how this had all been brought about— how they'd been working their job for Mr Douglas, the butcher, and how they'd overheard him speaking to a customer about the two of them, and about their mother. How she'd just died that day.

But, from what Imogen had thought, her mother had died giving birth to her and her brother.

Apparently, that wasn't the case.

When they'd confronted Douglas—all dressed up in his grease-soiled apron and with his forearms soaked with animal blood—he'd told them that their mother had abandoned the two of them, given them over to the Camp Council's care. And that, as a result, they'd ended up being tossed from person to person, to help out in whatever way they could to pay for the food which ended up in their mouths.

When she had pressed Douglas further, for some description about their mother, something which they *might* be able to hang onto, he had got vague . . . so vague, in fact, she hadn't believed a word of what he was telling them, and she wondered if he was simply playing a game.

In the end, she had managed to drag one fact from him, that

their mother—their *deceased* mother—had always worn a ring with a pair of entwined serpents.

Whether or not Imogen wanted to believe this, she couldn't say. But, with the knowledge that the Camp guards would be by at first light to set fire to the dead bodies from that day—the ones she and her brother were now scrabbling through—she had known that this was her and her brother's last chance to know the truth.

The *real* truth.

And so here they were.

Looking for the ring.

The confirmation that the mother they had never known— who had never wanted to know them—had indeed passed away. What she might do with that information, she had no idea.

She wouldn't know until she found her mother's body.

Together, she and Gut worked tirelessly through the seemingly endless bodies. They spoke no more. It was only when she felt the warmth on her back that she thought to look around. And there she saw—sure enough—the flaming glow of the sun just breeching the horizon. They didn't have time. No time at all.

When she looked back to Gut, he was staring over at her. She knew he wanted—more than anything—to scarper back to the Camp. If they left now they would surely be in time to start off at Douglas's shop, ready to help him sort the animal scraps into heaps for him to carve up.

But they couldn't go back.

Not yet.

There was still work to be done.

She worked with feverish energy, moving from one corpse to the next as if they weren't anything more than dead animals. She forgot completely they were dead *humans* . . . humans like her, and her brother.

The sun must've been up over the horizon for about fifteen

minutes when the glint caught her eye, when it sucked her in, showed her the way to just what she had been looking for. She scrabbled over the corpses and toward the light like some maddened magpie, and then bent down and looked.

The ring.

The entwined serpents.

She glanced back over her shoulder to her brother, but there was no need to call out to him. He was already there. With her. Together, they stared at the ring, still resting, wrapped about the finger of their dead mother. "What do we do?" Gut asked.

She could hear the fear in his voice—the way that his throat quivered. She looked down at the ring another time, and then, slowly, tracked her gaze back up the arm and to their mother's face.

Just as the other corpses were, her mother had her mouth wrenched open, a silent and ever-lasting scream echoing out through her lips. Her eyes were wide-open. Those same pale blue eyes that Imogen and her brother shared. They glinted in the rising sunlight.

She examined the ring, imagined herself, just about a million times, snatching it from her finger. But, in the end, she did nothing. She merely turned away and said—to Gut, "Come on."

Together, they headed off toward the trees which ran alongside the pile of bodies. There, in amongst the long grasses, the thickly packed together trees, they waited.

And they watched.

Ten minutes later, a group of guards appeared. They moved quietly, without speaking. In the fledgling sunlight, she made out the dark circles which hung down off their eyes. She knew they had spent the whole night on watch, keeping their eyes peeled as they surveyed the plains.

Each guard carried a torch, blazing away with its flame. They approached the pile of bodies. They busied themselves with a can of petrol, dousing the bodies with the strong-smelling liquid which made colourful patterns in the sunlight, and then, right as she prepared to draw a breath, one of the guards threw a match on top of it all.

At once, the bodies burst into dancing flames.

She stared at the spot where they'd found their mother—or where she *thought* their mother lay. For all she knew, she might have long ago lost sight of her.

Together, holding hands tightly, she sat still with her brother and they watched the guards leave and the flames lower themselves down to mere embers.

The pungent stench of burning flesh carried on the breeze, sent a nausea burrowing to the very pit of her gut. She clamped her teeth together, attempting to ward off the sensation. Then she grabbed hold of Gut's arm, dragged him deeper into the forest.

As she dragged him along, she heard him say, in a muffled voice which sounded—*to her*—submerged by tears, "What about the ring?"

She shook her head. "I never want to see it again."

After that, Gut slipped into silence and the two of them trudged on through the forest, and back toward the Camp. Douglas would be waiting for them. And there was no way their job would get done without them being there.

As they reached the collapsed wall—the way they had managed to escape the Camp and emerge onto the Plains—she ushered her brother through while she turned back to the dwindling embers.

She wasn't sure what she felt.

Guilt?

Despair?

A loss of her identity?

Perhaps there was a need for her to understand—to understand more about her mother. But, then again, as it always did out here, in the new world, understanding came *after* the need for survival.

And they needed to keep working to survive.

For now.

THE DEMENTED
PUPPETEER

THE INTERIOR seemed to stretch for miles into the gloom. Spry forms hung down from unseen hooks.

An incessant, mechanical *cluck* sounded.

For each footstep which wetly smacked against the floor, a light blinked on above.

Bright. White. Fluorescent.

It sent the darkness scurrying for the corners.

A figure emerged from the dawning, electronic day. He was dressed in a suit several sizes too large. It sagged off him like a scab ripe for picking. His gait was somewhere between a lope and a limp. Although he didn't walk with a cane, there was no doubt it would have aided his transit.

As the figure passed by the hanging forms, his face slowly caught the nascent light. His skin carried a light-blue hue. His eyes were sunken in their sockets—almost overwhelmed by shadow. He cast the odd side-long glance at the hanging forms—his *puppets*—and wondered, in the recesses of his mind, if there had ever been a mother created who'd felt such pride for her children, as the pride he felt now.

For his droids.

The figure—the *puppeteer*—arrived in the circle marked into the middle of an opening between the puppets. A screen protruded from the floor, its screen lit up with a bright, blue-white glow. The puppeteer approached. He stood over the device, his head angled down, eyes batting back and forth—reading, analysing, deciding.

His fingers sashayed across the screen, clearly seeing just as well as his eyes themselves saw. He worked his magic, just like a puppeteer manipulating strings. His hands becoming their hands.

His desires becoming *their* desires. It wasn't more than an electrical *whine* from out of the darkness. The first of many. It snapped his attention upward, away from the screen; a mere rendering of reality. He glanced about, blinking, making sense. Trying to fathom . . .

What had he done?

The puppeteer stood back from the screen. He peered off into the darkness.

He watched as the forms—*his puppets*—unfurled from their perches.

As they spread their arms.

As icy-white jets protruded from their articulations.

From the soles of their feet. From the heels of their hands.

They took to the air.

Hovering.

Holding off.

Waiting for the call.

The *final* call.

The *puppeteer's* call.

Almost without realising, the puppeteer raised his hand. Held them all so still. They remained captive to his spell. Unable to shift without his say-so . . .

Until he brought his hand downward.

And so ended the world.

CREEPING VINES,
SNAGGING FANGS

1

THE DARKNESS was a crippling weight. The air a mixture of sulphur and ash—ash which caught on the tongue and then plastered itself to the back of the throat.

A bitter asphyxiant.

Though there seemed to be sound all over, the only sure detail which could be identified was the screaming. That piercing shriek. And yet, it was so high-pitched, so scrapingly loud, that it was just above the capacity for hearing.

At least for human ears.

When Lawrie breathed in, she felt the dampness in her lungs, almost as if they were filling with some liquid which hung on the air. Her overalls were soaked and—when a light breeze blew—she could feel her skin trembling. Shaking away as it wrapped her light-weight, fragile, bird-boned body. Whenever she put one foot in front of the other, clinging to the moss-stricken, brick walls for balance, she felt as if the weight of the bulky, steel-capped boots she wore might be enough to pull her down. To pull her down for good.

And that would be the end of it.

Because she could hear *them* coming.

Although she couldn't hear much else but the screams in her ears, she was still certain that she *could* hear *them* coming.

As she took another step forward she felt her hand, smoothing its way along the wall, pass across something. Something sticking out. Something uneven.

She paused her advance.

Even though the darkness was complete, even though she had failed to follow the Wiseman's advice—had failed to cling to her sanity, to her real memories, to her real thoughts and her real opinions—she was sure that she could make out *something* sticking out from the wall. That was right, though, wasn't it? She still had those subconscious memories of the world. Those most basic of survival instincts. The ones which kept her *alive*.

Which *had* kept her alive.

Until now.

She moved her fingertips along the shaft of the object. It felt like metal. Knobbled, rusted-up metal. She felt her skin catch a few times against the oxidised spots. Felt that crawling sensation just beneath the surface of her skin.

Something . . . something about this . . . *this place* . . . about the lever . . . but—*oh, well*—it was all too late, because she gripped tight, and yanked it down.

Hard.

Before she knew it, she was falling.

Falling long.

And deeper into the darkness.

2

LAWRIE felt consciousness bleed back into her mind. When she breathed in the air, and tasted none of the choking ash or sulphur, when she heard nothing but a ringing sound in her ears —*no screaming!*—she felt as though her blood was tingling in her veins.

As though something was *inside* of her blood.

There was another thing, though, another thing which poked and prodded at her mind.

Light.

Sweet, and golden, and full of life.

It rose up seemingly miles away from her.

It illuminated some . . . were they really? . . . she could find no other explanation.

Other than they *had* to be clouds.

Soggy-bottomed, thick-to-bursting.

Clouds.

In the still-weak sunlight, she could outline their shapes. She could make out their blackish-blue tones. And, now, when she breathed in, she decided that what she could smell was *rain.* That slightly salty, slightly stale scent. All that water returning.

She reached about. Whatever it was that she lay on moved when she did. She reached down and felt the rough surface of . . . leaves? Yes, that was right, even in the half light—*so much better than all-consuming darkness!*—she could feel dried-up, crunchy leaves beneath her.

Without her willing, she felt her mind sketch back to some unconscious memory. To one of those which was forever lost. Which she would never be able to access if she had *wanted* to.

She pictured a small farmer's cottage. White walls. A thatched roof. A burbling little creek. She recalled several years. In the first she was small. A little girl. Crouched down on the bank of that creek. Dipping her fingers into the clear, flowing water. Feeling its coolness against her skin. And then she would bring her fingers up to her mouth. Suck the drops off.

Later, as her mind proceeded, older versions of herself repeated the action.

She could smell the freshly cut grass, the scent of the harvested hay carrying on the breeze. And she could taste—*always*—the very essence of the world. The *earth* on the tip of her tongue.

Until . . . until the last recollection which passed through her eyes.

When she couldn't any longer.

"They let you free then?"

The voice was gruff, uneven—*damaged* in some way.

Her heart leaped against her ribs. She felt every muscle in her body lock tight. She jerked her head around. Almost sank deeper into the pile of leaves on which she rested. Her eyes, so adjusted—if that was the word—to the dark, she could make out the shades of black. Could make out the form which lurked in the shadows surrounding her. Could tell that he was big, and heavy-set, and wearing a ragged coat. It had been so long since she had spoken, but she managed to speak now. " 'Free' ?"

In the notes of darkness which smothered the stranger whole, she identified the smiling, wide mouth of white teeth. For a pulsating second, she was certain that he was going to attack. Some sense within her—not memory, *deeper* than that—told her that he wanted to eat her.

That she was *unsafe*.

She scrabbled about, finally found something of the sturdy, *hard* ground, and pushed herself up.

At first, she stumbled about on her weakened legs—so used to being supported by the mossy, brick wall she'd hauled herself along back . . . back *there*.

"Mm-Hmm," the voice replied. "*Free as a bird.*"

Finally—*thankfully*—she managed to locate the rocky wall. She felt the rough surface against her skin. Her blood continued to tingle. She felt like her brain was fighting to crack open her skull from the inside. " 'Bird' ?" Lawrie repeated back at the voice.

"Yes, ma'am, just like a bird."

That triggered some sort of a recollection. It was when she stared outward, to the rising sun, and to the sprawling, *wild* landscape which surrounded her that she knew, on some gut level, that there were no birds here.

Not anymore.

There would never *be* anymore birds.

The light was now strong enough so that Lawrie could make out the outline of where she stood.

She could see the pile of leaves she had just got herself up and out of. And, a little beyond that, she could see *something*, a round, steel door plunged into the rock face.

An entrance into the underground.

Or so it seemed.

She turned her head in the direction of the voice. She could better make out the tattered overcoat which he wore now. All pockets—all *over* the place—and all of them seeming to be filled to bursting point.

As the light grew stronger still, she could make out little trinkets overspilling some of the pockets: twine, copper wire, scraps of paper.

"Don't you recognise me?" the voice asked.

She tried to concentrate. She attempted to clear all other thoughts from her mind.

But she failed.

If she forced them, the memories simply wouldn't come.

She shook her head.

"I," the voice said, "am the Wiseman."

3

LAWRIE LOOKED at the Wiseman with a cool glare, as if she should feel some kind of a rising, uncontrollable emotion within. But she couldn't tell *how* she should feel. If she should feel the bubbling lava of anger churning away in her stomach, or feel some cool cut of jealousy. The dizzy nausea of confusion dominated.

Her mouth tasted strongly of moss still. From those times when she had given up. When she had realised her strength had been entirely depleted. And she had simply *had* to fill her mouth— her stomach—with something or other. And all that'd been available, aside from the bricks or the leather of her shoes, had been the moss.

The Wiseman was dark skinned, though he had a pinkish glow where his blood kissed the surface. He held himself upright, straight-backed, and he stood *so* tall . . . and yet Lawrie was convinced that, if she wanted to, if she ran at him flat out, she could knock him onto his back without much trouble.

He was all show.

A sham.

Lies about strength.

"Where am I?" Lawrie asked, her voice quivering slightly.

Another smile from the Wiseman. That clean, *cutting* outline of white teeth. "You're back among the living, Lawrie, you're back in the *real* world."

She stared down over herself. She took in the grey-white overalls she wore: now covered in sweat, and grease and mud, and earth . . . and who knew what else.

When she reached for the zipper of her overalls, she found that it was thick with rust. With a couple of tugs, she managed to work it free. She dragged it down a little way with a flat, ugly *ziiip* then, still feeling the Wiseman's eyes upon her, she stopped.

She stared back.

"I don't remember anything," she said.

The Wiseman's smile widened. "No, I don't suppose you do. But, really, that's the point, don't you think?"

"I don't *think* anything."

"Well, my mother always told me that whenever I was trying to find something I should think about the very last place I seen it."

Lawrie felt her chest tighten. She was certainly getting angry now. "I don't remember *anything*."

"Sure thing," he said, with a slight chuckle. "Then I'd say you're in one hell of a pickle."

She stared long and hard at him. Then she turned away, looked out over the scenery now becoming illuminated by the rising sun. She caught the outlines of the trees, and, a little beyond that, the long grasses of a glade, each blade seemingly withering up and out, reaching up for the sun as if its rays would bring healing.

When she turned back to the Wiseman, she felt as if her mind was feeding her little morsels. Nothing more than *fragments* but better than nothing. Better than what she had had before. "The world," she said. "The world's *sick*."

The Wiseman chuckled again. He shook his head. Then he took a couple of steps forward.

She noticed how he limped, and she wondered why she had so honed in on that particular detail. Why didn't he have a cane— some sort of a walking aid? Or had he . . . something spoke to her . . . . *nudged her* . . . suggested that he had lost it, somehow.

The Wiseman halted at some prearranged point. Then he reached out his hand, his slightly crooked fingers unfurling from the ends of his thick-wristed arms. "You see? Out there?"

She followed where he indicated. She squinted, finding the

sunlight which glowed all around now made the world almost too bright to look at. As if it might blind her if she allowed it to . . . and it was then she felt the harshest, most rebellious voice which she had yet encountered. The one telling her—no, *shouting* at her—that she would, never again, allow herself to experience pain.

That she would never get herself entangled in the troubles with which she had fought back . . . *there*.

In the distance, she just managed to pick out the outline of some building. It was grey, made of cement, and had unsightly, rusted metal poles jutting out of it.

Something caused her heart to lift.

That sense of . . . of *home*.

She felt the Wiseman take a couple of steps and arrive at her side. His limp seemed more obvious now, as if he wasn't any longer taking pains to hide it.

As she felt the memories tumbling through her—*too-narrow*—mind's eye, she said, "Where am I? Where am I? What does all of this *mean*?"

The Wiseman remained quiet for several moments. Then, when he replied in his thick, deep voice, she could tell he was no longer smiling. "I did think that pertinent questions might well be the Order of the Day." He turned his head to her, examining her in profile. "Why don't you just come along with me?"

4

LAWRIE WAS SURPRISED by the Wiseman's ability for navigating through every given obstacle. It wasn't that he was fast, or that he had any particularly efficient manoeuvrability, but he made steady progress. And without catching his foot on a stray tree root, or on any of the creeping vines which snaked across their path. Which was less than could be said for Lawrie herself.

So accustomed was she to trudging across the sturdy, brick floor of the maze that she found the softer ground unwieldy. She found her boots sinking in if she stopped too soon, for breath, or to check on where it was she and the Wiseman were headed.

In the end, she decided only to follow on the Wiseman's heels.

To *trust* him with their destination.

Because he claimed he knew where they were headed.

Finally, after what must've been several hours, the sun was fully launched into the sky. It hung at its highest point, sending its warmth down, and its baking rays back up through the ground they passed over. Their only cover was the canopy of the trees they passed beneath.

The Wiseman led her out of the trees, and onto the plains.

Thick with long grass.

There, standing before them, dominating the whole landscape, was the dilapidated building which she had first seen up on that ledge, where she had awoken in that pile of dried-up leaves.

The Wiseman did not pause to explain, or even to allow Lawrie to try and reassemble something of what this building actually *meant* to her in her mind.

A rotted wooden door covered only the middle section of the opening. Its handle had turned a shade of green from rust. But the Wiseman did not hesitate as he reached out to turn it.

To let the two of them inside.

The air here smelled strongly of tree bark, and of some plastic component, something which Lawrie might've termed 'unnatural'. She noted the little gas stove which sat near the entrance of the building. She saw the saucepan—just as rusted up as the doorknob —and the ashen glob of food which stuck to its base. She glanced to the Wiseman, as if he might be able to feed her some sort of an explanation. But his only explanation was that knowing smile of his.

He led her up a set of spiralling stairs.

With each step, Lawrie was almost certain that she was twisting her gut a little more. All the way, until she felt as if she couldn't tighten it any further. She felt that the motion of her movement upward and around might suck her in. But, before she could totally lose her mind to this sensation, the Wiseman brought them to the top of the staircase.

Lawrie found herself staring out across a mostly bare room— nothing but a cement floor, just like all the other rooms in this building. There was a sodden mattress shoved up against one wall. And there was a pile of battered old books beside it too. And a metal torch with a large dent in its side which, she now—*instinctively*—knew she had used to read at night.

The Wiseman stood back, as if to give her space to take in the room, to allow her memories to swirl about in her brain so that they might—*finally*—come clear.

She trod over the cement floor. She glanced about. There was nothing else in this space. Just the glassless window which peered on out over their surroundings.

Which, surely, looked back to where they had just come from.

That large hill which erupted out from the trees.

Could she see a faint glimmer of sunlight reflected off the round metal door?

When she turned back into the room, she hoped that she might be able to remember it all. But she couldn't shift any such recollection through her mind. There was nothing for her to get her fingernails dug into. It was as if she was attempting to catch tiny fish in a stream using nothing but a sieve full of large holes. All recollection simply poured out through the holes.

Gone forever.

"Do you remember now? Anything at all?"

Lawrie shook her head. She couldn't lie to him. There *wasn't* anything for her to tell him. She remembered nothing at all. The pieces just wouldn't fit.

She heard the Wiseman give a heavy sigh.

As if he was disappointed in her.

But what was *she* supposed to do?

She felt like crying, but she held herself back.

"We been together a long time, that's what hurts," the Wiseman said. "That's what hurts the most about it."

All of a sudden, she felt the rage grip her. She felt as if some switch had been flipped in her brain. Anger—*anger which she had never thought herself capable of*—poured through her, lapping and lashing, thick and bursting and impossible to control.

She rushed the Wiseman.

Caught him off balance.

Knocked him back.

Those moments were long as she drank in the wide—*wide*—whites of his eyes.

As she watched them watching him.

They fell onto the cement floor with a *thud*.

And she felt something within the Wiseman breaking.

Some important part.

Something *unfixable*.

As she rolled off his chest, she watched the Wiseman writhe, and roll, from one side to the other, unable to keep up his cool exterior any longer. "Tell me," she said, her voice cool, calm, and then repeated, *"Tell me!"* this time all insistence, the threat of another strike hanging over the Wiseman.

The Wiseman screwed up his eyes. He curled his body away from her.

Lawrie knew that it hadn't been all her.

That it hadn't been something so simple as a well-placed blow to his gut.

No, there was something else dwelling within the Wiseman.

Something else which *ailed* him.

She had just been the one to push him over the edge.

The Wiseman crushed his eyes together. She watched as a single tear squeezed itself out and rolled down his cheek. When he spoke, he babbled a little, as if his own blood might be surging up his throat, *choking* him. "There was . . . a . . . a *community* . . . they were . . . were . . ."

Since he couldn't find the words, he scrapped together the strength to lift his arm and point off out the window, through the trees.

She crouched over him, seeing the fright in his eyes, that look which told her, without misinterpretation, that death was closing in on him now. That it would soon be upon him.

The Wiseman found his voice again. "Some . . . some *army* . . . they wanted us dead . . . wanted us *all* dead . . . you went in there . . . with the, the . . . that . . ."

Here he pointed at Lawrie's belt.

She didn't understand what he was getting at.

Not at all.

Finally, the whites of the Wiseman's eyes locked onto hers. *"Gas,"* he said. *"Gas."* Here he managed a grim smile. "Knocked the sense out of them, you did. Knocked them all into blubbering morons . . . guess you . . . you got a bit too much of it . . . was only meant to make you . . . make you forget a little . . . a little while at the most."

She felt about for some recognition. Something within herself telling her whether this was all truth, or if it was a lie. She couldn't much tell anymore. She supposed that he could tell her just about anything he wanted and she would be none the closer to knowing the truth.

She stood.

She stared down at the Wiseman.

His eyes swivelled up to her. "Please," he said, his voice now gasping, "please don't leave me . . . don't leave me to die *alone*."

But she was already treading carefully across the room.

Headed for the spiral staircase which led down.

Leaving him behind.

5

D OWNSTAIRS, in the building, Lawrie had managed to scrape together a few supplies. She had also located a rucksack—one of those military-issue, beige numbers. It had several tears, but most of them were in places it didn't matter. She found food: can upon can of carrots, and beans, and other such items. She stuffed all she felt she could carry into the rucksack.

On her way out of the building, she surprised herself in standing for a long while in the doorway. She didn't know what she was waiting for. Maybe she just wanted to pause to hear the Wiseman's cracked cries for help which floated down the staircase.

Or perhaps she just wanted to remember *something* about what had gone on.

But, she was decided, the time for remembering was long gone.

Once outside, she simply picked a direction and hiked. She walked on into the falling night, feeling that she was doing all that she could. That she was doing the *right thing*. Now that she had no memory she could not trust anything.

Or *anyone*.

With the last remaining scraps of daylight, she came upon a chain-link fence. When she stepped up to it, through the thick grass which grew about its base, she noted where it had been cut. Where people had cut their way through.

She eased the rucksack off over her shoulder and passed it through one of the gaps. Then she ducked under, and through, doing her best to avoid the snagging fangs of the cut-off pieces of wire.

She had had enough horror.

It was a whole new world now.

As she passed through to the other side of the fence, she looked back. And she saw the sign: peeled by the elements, faded by the sun. Its message was clear, *unambiguous* . . . even to a child it would've been that way:

Military Exclusion Zone: Do Not Enter

Though she didn't right away know why she paused to stare for so long at the sign, she decided later, when she made camp in a set of quite comfortable caves, that she was just trying to trigger something. Some memory. *Some* aspect of the past.

Had she been used as a tool?

Some kind of blunt instrument for human suffering?

For torture?

But there really was nothing.

As she brought the blanket up to her throat—a blanket she'd stuffed into the rucksack earlier—she felt the warm material working its magic, keeping out the cold.

She realised that it no longer mattered.

That she would live in the present moment from now on.

And she would do things her way.

Even if it got her killed.

LAST ONE ALIVE

1

JAY FISHLEY saunters along the row of vidscreens taking his time to examine each image. He looks for definition, sharpness and clarity of image. He tries to take on the appearance of any other consumer, come here to do a spot of shopping, but, in truth, this is the first time he's been out of his flat in days. Every second he's out here he feels his muscles knot up more, his heart clunk harder and faster against his ribcage.

As he scans along the rows, he takes in a football match—the drone players sweeping back and forth with the ball bobbing between them, meanwhile a tickertape runs across the base of the screen offering gambling odds at the brush of a fingertip. This vidscreen being a shop model, however, Jay knows that feature will be disabled. If he wished to bet on the game he would need to buy the device, have his fingerprints assigned to it through Host.

He looks at the other screens: a soap opera, replete with all the usual concerns—the extra-terrestrial relationship, a Staruk breaking up with an earthling. On the next, a game show takes place with a series of garish, multi-coloured flashing pink and purple lights. There's no moment to breathe as the host prattles through, guiding the gormless contestants from one phase to the next. This is all overwhelming and gets to Jay's head—makes his brain squelch and nausea seep through him. It's time to go back home.

As he turns to leave the shop, he finds himself face-to-face with an assistant, blocking his path. An earthling, like him. She has bright blue eyes—clearly engineered at a drop-in clinic—and fresh, rose-red lips. Her complexion is white as snow and her hair black as night. Again, these features are no freak of nature.

"May I help you, sir?" she says, her badge, with the shop's

name *Sparks* written out in a burst of purple at the top, reveals her name to be Rita, and 'Glad to be of service.'

Jay tears himself away from those laser eyes. "I'm just looking," he says. "In fact, I was just about to go."

She makes no move to unblock his path—no doubt on orders to contain all prospective customers, to steer them, item in hand, to the cash register. "I see you've been looking at the vidscreens. Has anything in particular caught your eye?"

He keeps his face hidden from her, remaining in profile, eyes fixed on the game show, trying his best to look interested in whatever it is that the host has to say.

"Sir?" she says. "Are you all right? You look a little—"

This time he turns to her and when he speaks it's with a snap in his tone. "I'm fine, okay? Just leave me alone, won't you?"

He admonishes himself for losing his temper and mumbles an apology. The assistant, however, keeps up her bright and easy smile. Perhaps she's accustomed to volatile customers—beings from other planets with a lesser grasp of human manners. "Maybe I can interest you in the Phoenix Three," she says, as she rotates her body and indicates a vidscreen, flashing away in the air. She twizzles her fingers and the screen expands to three times its previous size, to occupy the space between them—the game show in which Jay had feigned captivation plays out in gigantic detail. "Do you see the attention to detail in the skin tones?" she says, indicating the host's forehead with her index finger.

"Yes, yes," Jay says, looking away from the screen and to the exit.

She leaves the screen there for another second or so before minimising it. She looks him over and then her hands go to her lips, parted with shock. "You're . . . you're him, aren't you?"

Jay glances round. There's no way out of the shop, short of barrelling past the assistant, and for all her heavy-handed salesmanship, he doesn't want to hurt her, not for something so minor as saving face. And so he relaxes his shoulders and looks at her, readying himself for the same routine all over again.

"You were on TV."

"Yes," he says, "that's right."

"I saw you on the vidscreen, being interviewed on Central One. No one ever gets onto Central One."

Jay's heart beats quicker. This has been a big mistake. Why didn't he just stay in his flat? What made him think that this all would've blown over, that he would've been able to go out into the street without being recognised?

She gets closer still and then reaches out to touch his cheek. "I never thought I'd ever meet someone who'd been on Central One."

He flinches at her touch, but resists the urge to rush past her, to beat a hasty retreat through the shop and out into the street. Such rash action would surely bring the security drones' attention to him, and then he would have all the explaining to do—more people would gather, desperate to know how he had got onto Central One.

Seeing that she's affecting him with her touching his cheek, she draws back, but none of her curiosity wanes. "What was it like to be on Central One?"

Jay's palms sweat. "Oh, I don't know. It really wasn't anything special."

Her eyes gape. "Not special? How can you say that? Why, I don't know anyone who doesn't dream of making Central One. My aunt, she managed to make Central Seventeen a while ago, but it was nothing special"—she nods her head to the Phoenix Three, its screen now reduced to a normal size, no bigger than a small window—"just a silly, unwatched game show."

"I see," Jay says, trying to work out his escape route.

She brightens a touch. "Say, wouldn't you come back home

with me, to meet my aunt? She would absolutely love to meet someone who's been on Central One. What do you say?"

"No, I really can't. I've got lots to do this afternoon."

"Oh please, I'll make it worth your while, make you tea—we've got some of the unfrozen kind. We've been saving it for a special occasion."

Jay attempts to round her, to get by along the shelf, past the flickering vidscreens.

Rita stays in his path, head cocked slightly to one side, her eyes pleading. "It won't take long, and it'll mean the universe to my aunt. She'll never forgive me if I tell her I bumped into someone who was on Central One and didn't invite them back home."

"Then don't tell her," Jay says, then with a light shove manages to get by the girl.

Approximately three steps later she bursts out into a piercing wail.

Jay pirouettes and glares back, almost unable to believe what he's witnessing. She's actually crying at the prospect of him walking away, leaving her here. He gazes over the shop floor. One of the security drones points in their direction, the lens of its camera whirring away. He takes the decision and returns to the girl's side.

Despite all her heavy cosmetic work—the surgically enhanced features—he can see that below all that she was once quite pretty, in a dormouse, girl-next-door kind of way. He reaches out and touches her shoulder, giving it a light squeeze. "Um, are you okay?"

She sobs away some more.

He glances back over the shelves to the security drone. It hovers on at the door, bobbing lightly. He needs to get out of here pretty sharpish. A scene is the last thing he wants. Once again he curses having left his flat. He should've just stayed put, been content in his boredom, and safety.

A large, middle-aged lady with frizzy brown hair appears at Jay's heels. She wears a purple jacket, matching the branding colours of the shop. She has all the hallmarks of a boss. "What's the matter here?" she says.

The girl sobs on, so it's left up to Jay for an explanation.

"It's just—" he says.

"Hey, I know you! Weren't you on Central One?"

"No, I think you're mistaking me for someone else."

She squints then cracks a smile. "I'm sure you're him, you know—"

Jay puts his arm around the girl. "Look, is it all right if . . ." he pauses, not being able to see her nametag, then continues, ". . . it's just that she's in a bit of a state. Can she have the afternoon off?"

All the jubilation leaks out of the woman, like air dribbling out of a helium balloon. Her shoulders go slack and she places her hands on her hips. "All right, she is looking a bit on the fragile side, and trade's not exactly roaring this afternoon." She bends forward, giving him a glimpse of her cleavage. "You get some rest, eh, Rita. Come in tomorrow all freshened up."

"Thank you," Jay says, putting his arm around the girl, who's still sniffling away, and shepherding her toward the exit.

As he goes past the woman, she says, "It is you, though, isn't it? You're really him?"

"Yes, I am."

2

RITA STOPS sobbing when they reach her local magnet rail station.

Jay does consider whether he might be able to leave her behind, to go off and sneak back to his flat, but now that he's come this far, and Rita's feeling better about herself, he decides that a cup of tea might be just what he needs. The fact that it's *real* tea swings it.

And so they get off together and venture along the raised platform, Level Forty-One, which is steadily lit with neon lights stitched into plastic palm trees. The colour of the glow changes every couple of seconds: from a light, soothing green, to a calming blue. All this is designed to keep the inhabitants docile, free of painful thoughts.

Doors spring up either side of them. A single black keypad is stuck at each entrance, a tiny red light awaiting a finger to scan. Rita struts up to one of the doors and sticks her finger onto the scanner. The red light changes to green and the door slides upward. She beckons for Jay to follow.

The flat smells lightly of peach. Jay spots the fragrance module beside the front door and sees that it's tuned to 'Summer Fruits.' He never uses the fragrance module in his own flat, unable to get past the queasiness in his stomach, the deep-set knowledge that what he's smelling is a manufactured odour. He just likes to leave his flat as it is—to leave the odour neutraliser to its own devices with nothing to take the edge off its sharp scent.

"Make yourself comfortable," Rita says, tottering off toward— what Jay presumes to be—the kitchen.

He surveys the lounge setup. A sofa and two easy chairs. There's a wilting rose sticking up out of a thin, glass vase on the coffee table. He inches closer, inspects it and proclaims it false at a second glance. The colouration is too perfect. It reminds him of Rita's face.

Rita bobs out of the kitchen with a hover tray following in her wake. The tray deposits itself on the coffee table, taking care not to bump into the pseudo rose. A pair of glasses containing a colourless liquid perch atop the table.

"Is that—?"

"Yes," she says, with a grin. "Fresh water, straight from the Noral Mountains, mined from an unaffected spring, well beneath the surface."

Unable to believe this, Jay raises the glass and inspects it with a more discerning eye. No trace of contamination. Incredible. Not even the tell-tale sign of purification, the green tone. It's real, which is more than can be said for the rose. "It must've cost a fortune," he says, putting the glass back down.

"Take a sip," she says.

He looks to the water again, picks it up and then, with the edge of the glass pressing against his lower-lip, he hesitates, attempts to breathe in its smell, but all he gets is ersatz peaches. Realising this is the closest he's ever going to get to drinking the real thing, he sips.

"I'd been saving it for a special occasion."

"Thank you," he says, replacing the near-untouched glass back on the coffee table. "Really, I'm honoured."

She giggles and her cheeks flush pink in perfect unison—blush implants.

Is there *anything* about her that's real?

"We're the ones who should be honoured," she says, "having someone like you in our flat."

Jay has almost forgotten that he's here to meet Rita's aunt, to be presented as living, breathing evidence that *real* people can make it onto Central One. And, once again, he feels uncomfortable about the idea, gets a fresh urge to venture back home to his flat. But this . . . the water now and the tea to come, he can hardly duck out, can he?

Before he gets the chance to think any further, the front door swishes open and Rita rushes to her feet and dances along the hall to welcome her aunt home.

Jay gets to his feet, ready again for this grating, minor-celebrity routine.

Rita's aunt's eyes shift round the lounge as she darkens the doorway, Rita just at her heels. If Jay hadn't known better he might've believed her to be Rita's mother. They share just the same features: the black hair, the white skin, the incredibly blue eyes. Maybe they went to the same drop-in clinic. Rita's aunt wears a well-cut, grey trouser suit. If Jay had to guess he would say that she's returning home from some lower-level government office job where she works as an information proofer or, perhaps, as a drone programmer.

Rita's aunt's eyes widen and she takes Jay in, as if drinking him in with her glare. She comes within a matter of centimetres, without speaking, her breath hot on Jay's face and then, out of nowhere, says, "You're *him*. You really did it. You were on Central One."

Jay has no idea what he's supposed to say to this claim, so he simply nods his head.

She slips her bag strap down over her arm and deposits the bag itself at her feet. A maintenance drone scurries out from one of the ventilation flaps and retrieves the bag, shooting off through a forest of legs and out of sight. The *snap* of another ventilation flap shutting off in the distance of the flat seems to bring Rita's aunt back to life.

"My name's Emma," she says, breaking out into a toothy grin—

a computer-designed smile—and then showing Jay to the sofa. Within a few voice commands a screen materialises before their eyes. Jay locates the generator in the corner of the room, a Phoenix Three. He supposes that Rita, working at Sparks, is entitled to some sort of discount on its products. At least he knows that her salesmanship was genuine—that she was pushing a product she's glad to use herself, in her own home.

Rita sits the other side of Jay, and he finds himself there, sandwiched between aunt and niece. The screen sweeps through its navigation screens, controlled by Emma's eye movements. She has the system run a scan on Jay's facial profile, and the appropriate clip flashes up on screen, paused at the moment where Jay's face first appeared on Central One.

Both Rita and Emma run their eyes over him, then Emma commands the clip to play.

It's a funny feeling, watching himself there, squirming away on the sofa while Richard Bandjeck—the renowned talk show host—spits questions at him, asks him to reel through the whole account, from start to finish, only to cut Jay off whenever he gets into the flow of the story. Bandjeck asks about how Jay feels for surviving a disaster where everybody else has died and if he has any guilt knowing that many families were not so fortunate. The on-screen Jay does his best to dodge through the questions, under pressure from Bandjeck to get a move on—to wrap them up quickly and succinctly in a way that will mean Bandjeck can get on with the show, move onto his interview with a Horned Kirvner—the newest alien to be added to the record of human space exploration. Jay wonders when the loss of human life was superseded, in news outlets, by the discovery of new life forms, and then wonders whether or not it's a bad thing.

Under pressure from the director to cut to an advertisement break, Jay clearly remembers the jerky movements off camera,

Bandjeck lurches forward in his seat and grasps Jay's hand in his, thanks him for coming onto the show and wishes him a safe journey home. Relieved, Jay exits, stage left.

The screen jerks to a halt and the menu reappears asking Emma what she would like to do next, whether she would like to search for another facial profile or, perhaps, search for some appropriate viewing matter from within her preferred archives. Emma blinks twice and the reel goes back to the start.

Still clearly in a daze following the viewing, Rita rises to her feet, swaying slightly as she heads for the kitchen. "I'll go and make the tea," she says.

Jay's limbs stiffen as he observes himself on Central One, his face in freeze frame, wrinkles marking his forehead and the area around his eyes—giveaway signs of his extreme anxiety. And so he remains there, condemned to reliving his appearance on *Bandjeck Chats*, yet again.

3

THEY WATCH the footage again and again. Jay takes his tea and slurps away at it, enjoying the rich flavour, completely different from the frozen type. The effect of the caffeine feels much greater, perking him into action, telling him that he must be reaching a tipping point in his life—that he's not going to live out the rest of his life through this seven-minute clip of a TV show, because despite all the exposure he still hasn't been able to tell his story. Not really.

Rita collects the cups of tea and places them on the hover tray, which jets off into the kitchen to deposit them, in turn, into the automatic dishwasher, then she lets out a long and steady yawn, covering her mouth with her perfectly manicured hand. "Well, I can't be the only one who's a little tired."

Catching the yawning disease, Emma does the same. She triple blinks and the projection returns to the home screen, then she gives the voice command for it to switch off.

Jay's raring to get out of the flat, away from these two woman and back to the safety of his own flat, but, just as he finds the perfect moment to make his excuses, and beat a hasty retreat, Emma touches him on the arm.

"Please," she says, "you've got to get us onto Central One."

Jay feels a little foggy, that seven-minute clip of his embossed on his brain. "Huh?"

"You know Bandjeck," Rita says, "you can find a way to get us on."

"But, how, what? I don't understand, sorry."

Emma continues, "A soap opera, a dramatization, maybe, just something we can get our teeth into. A start, that's all we're asking for."

The whole preposition is so absurd that Jay fights the temptation to laugh in their faces. But he recalls that they're his hosts, they've been kind to him, indulged him with tea and fresh water—all they've done wrong is to smother him with that damn broadcast.

Trying his best to dampen the situation, Jay gets up from the sofa and makes for the door. Neither Emma or Rita make to stop him. When he reaches the door, he says, "Thanks for everything." Outside he takes five paces before breaking out into a run and heading for the magnet railway station.

As he rolls up to the barrier, he's confronted with the fingerprint scanner, he looks around and considers his situation. It's probably okay. Most likely no one's watching him. No one will pop up asking him about that *damn* Central One If he does it quickly he'll be on the next train, here any minute now. Still, despite all his rationalisation, he hesitates and that's all it takes for a drone to pop up in his face.

"Is everything all right, sir?" it says, in its synthesised voice.

A quiver passes through his stomach. "Yes, fine."

"Please place your right index finger against the scanner."

Jay eyes the scanner and then his finger. He presses it onto the surface, smoothed into a convex dip from all the times it's been used. The light swoops along his finger, taking the data and sending it off to some sub-section of Host for analysis. With a satisfied *blip*, the turnstile gives way and Jay proceeds through to the other side.

"Have a nice journey, sir."

The drone's voice startles Jay, and then he realises that he can go, that he can get on his train and get back to his flat, away from all this craziness.

As he waits on the platform, the virtual map—like mist hanging before his eyes—reveals the location of the next magnet train, about ten minutes off yet. He drums his fingers against his thigh and watches the map intently, as if he might be able to speed up the train by simple power of will.

The drone hovers along the platform, just above the edge of the rails, scanning everything, processing the information, sending off to Host, and then repeating. When it reaches Jay it halts and scans him once more. Then it waits, silently.

Jay stares into the tinted lens which operates as its eye. His image is being broken up into a series of ones and zeroes and sent through Host. Sometimes he wishes that drones would have some sense of social etiquette—it not being entirely becoming to loom over someone, staring intently at them.

After the drone has spent several minutes in front of Jay, he sucks up the courage to say something. "Look here," he says, "I'm just waiting for the train to get back home. Can't you leave me in peace?"

The drone whirs to itself.

"What do you want?"

The drone remains silent another moment then says, "I have found a record of your facial profile on a transmission through Central One. You appeared on the show entitled: *Bandjeck Chats* on—"

Jay waves his hands in front of the drone. "I know, I know! Do you think that I need to be told that when everyone's recognising me everyday? Isn't it enough that humans come up to me asking if I'm *the one*, without having drones bother me too?"

The drone hums to itself.

He feels a sob welling at the back of his throat. Looking round, seeing that he's completely alone on this platform, it being well after tenth hour, he has no resilience left and he breaks down into uncontrollable weeping.

The drone burbles something.

He swishes his hand in its direction, trying to swat it like a gigantic fly, then he presses his head into his hands and digs his fingernails into his scalp. "Leave me alone!"

The magnet train rumbles through the tunnel and then hisses up to the platform.

"You see?" Jay says. "That's my ride home. I'm just a normal person, I've done nothing to deserve this, to have to walk around like some sort of third-rate celebrity."

The drone still ticks away to itself.

Jay suppresses a swearword, knowing that making trouble with the drone will lead to greater problems with the authorities— police knocking on the door of his flat in the middle of the night and taking him away for a stern talking to. At the very least.

The drone hangs there.

Jay makes for the magnet train, its doors yawning open.

"Why don't you tell me your story."

Jay pivots and stares back at the drone. "What?" he says. "What did you say?"

"Your story. Would you tell me what really happened?"

Jay remains stunned, unable to believe the ridiculousness of the situation, that this drone is actually asking *him* to tell the story. He glances into the magnet train, seeing one of the spongy blue seats within, inviting him inside, to take the ride back home. But he hesitates, one foot on the step leading into the carriage.

Another synthesised voice, this time of the computer system driving the train says, "Please clear obstruction."

Jay lingers another moment and then, mind made up, steps off the magnet train. He sizes up the drone as the magnet train thrums off behind him, picking up speed and then disappearing into the pitch black tunnel.

The drone stays where it is—its tinted camera lens still fixed on Jay.

"Do you really want to know?" Jay says.

The drone hums to itself.

Jay allows himself a smile and then starts to tell his story—right from the start, just like it happened.

BETTER EARTH (TM)
WORLD BUILDER

P LEASE SELECT your starting biome.
     Briggits-B has selected SNOWY MOUNTAINS.
A series of mountainous valleys, sapling forests and sprouting shoots appears before you. Slowly this landscape transforms before your eyes. The branches twist their way up to the sky. The trunks thicken. Shoots take the form of bushes. And foliage. The world stands before you, verdant, and ready for inhabitation.

Your humanoid replica appears on screen.

You need food, shelter, and drinking water.

Please select your initial path for exploration.

Briggits-B has selected WALK FORWARD.

When you venture out into the snow, it quickly freezes the soles of your feet. A little while later frostbite sets in.

I'm sorry. You are dead.

Thank you for using the BetterEarth™ World Builder.

———

Please select your starting biome.

Tesseral-14 has selected RAINFOREST.

The ground remains flat, extremely fertile, and before you endless saplings and sprouts jut out from the earth. They point up toward the sky. Many bear fruits and nuts. Within the plant life there starts many creature lifecycles.

Your humanoid replica appears on screen.

You need food, shelter, and drinking water.

Please select your initial path for exploration.

Tesseral-14 has selected WALK FORWARD.

When you venture into the jungle, sounds fill your ears, and the fallen branches and leaves crunch beneath your feet. The ground is a little muddy and you can feel it suck with each step. Chirruping sounds through the trees. Many animals reside here.

You come across a rushing stream of what appears to be clear water.

Please select your action.

Tesseral-14 has selected DRINK WATER.

You dip your hands into the stream, forming a seal with them so that the water shall not spill. You drink from your hands.

Your thirst has been quenched.

You need food and shelter.

Please select your path for exploration.

Tesseral-14 has selected GO RIGHT.

You turn around and pass through a pair of trees. The path continues to be muddy beneath your feet. It weighs you down. Tires you.

Prioritise food?

Tesseral-14 has selected YES.

When you turn your attention to the jungle which surrounds you, it is impossible to see anything that might be camouflaged. There are animal sounds all around, but the source of these sounds is not apparent.

Your hunger causes your stomach to rumble.

Do you wish to continue WALKING?

Tesseral-14 has selected YES.

The heat grows thicker still. Much harder to stand. The water with which you only recently quenched your thirst now seeps out through your skin. You glance about. Hope for something to catch your attention. An easy kill. Some prey.

Up ahead, you spy a boar.

Please select your action.

Tesseral-14 has selected CHASE BOAR.

You put one foot after the other. You pursue the boar. The boar tilts its head up. Catches sight of you. And then it runs.

The boar escapes.

You need food and shelter.

Your stomach rumbles and you feel weak.

Prioritise food?

Tesseral-14 has selected YES.

The jungle continues to sprawl away from you on all sides. It is a constantly moving canvas of rich greens and nourishing browns. There is a bush with red berries at your feet.

Please select your action.

Tesseral-14 has selected EAT BERRIES.

In a fit of hunger, you rip the berries off the plant and shovel them in past your lips. You chew on the berries. Their juice is sour. Almost too sour to swallow. But you swallow them. They burn down your throat. And then they burn your belly.

They keep burning.

They never stop burning.

I'm sorry. You are dead.

Thank you for using the BetterEarth^{TM} World Builder.

————

Please select your starting biome.

Harbrunger7Star has selected PLAINS.

Long grasses poke up through the earth. They mature and wave in the wind. A warming sun beats down on the landscape. A little way out across the plains, animals are created. They take on form. They ease their way into the landscape.

Your humanoid replica appears on screen.

You need food, shelter, and drinking water.

Please select your initial path for exploration.

Harbrunger7Star has chosen GO BACKWARD.

You turn around to find a gentle hill growing up out of the terrain. The long grasses conceal the earth beneath. The sun remains warm. Not hot. A small pond awaits before you with a fresh flowing stream running into it.

Please select your action.

Harbrunger7Star has selected DRINK WATER.

You dip your hands into the stream, forming a seal with them so that the water shall not spill. You drink from your hands.

Your thirst has been quenched.

You need food and shelter.

Please select your path for exploration.

Harbrunger7Star has selected GO LEFT.

You venture into the long grasses and come across a rabbit carcass half-buried.

The carcass is fresh and has a clean bite mark across the throat.

Please select your action.

Harbrunger7Star has selected EAT CARCASS.

You eat through the carcass. Its entrails and blood dribble down your chin. In a little while, a gentle warmth passes through you as your stomach becomes contented with the meal.

You need shelter.

Please select your path for exploration.

Harbrunger7Star has selected GO FORWARD.

You pass through the long grasses. Ahead you catch sight of a log—fallen onto the long grasses. You venture closer. The log has moss clotted up its sides. Growing from its bark.

Please select your action.

Harbrunger7Star has selected BREAK LOG APART.

You have broken the log apart.

Please select your action.

Harbrunger7Star has selected **CREATE SHELTER FROM LOG**.

You work quickly, crafting the broken pieces into easily malleable resources. You work all day and into some of the night. When you have finished, the shelter shall be sufficient to keep you sheltered from the cold.

You need sleep.

Please select your action.

Harbrunger7Star has selected **GO TO SLEEP**.

You sleep long into the night, and into the early-morning hours. Before the sun rises, a chill runs through your shelter. It stirs your naked body. You rise up and rub your arms over your chest. But your trembling continues.

You need warmth.

Please select your action.

Harbrunger7Star has selected **FIND CARCASS**.

For many hours, you stumble through the long grasses. Finally, when the sun rises over the horizon, you find the remains of the carcass. But it is insufficient to create any sort of clothes. You leave the carcass alone.

Please select your path for exploration.

Harbrunger7Star has selected **GO FORWARD**.

You move further into the plains. The long grasses continue to grow up at either side of you. Your chill from the night before worsens. It causes your blood to thicken. For your forehead to feel weighty and matted. You fall to your knees, coughing and sneezing.

Night returns.

A pack of wolves feasts on your sickened, naked form.

I'm sorry. You are dead.

Thank you for using the BetterEarth^{TM} World Builder.

———

Please select your starting biome.

WereAllDoomed4000 has selected VOLCANIC.

The landscape grows up to form rough, grey slightly red-tinged earth. You can feel vibrations passing through your feet, and up through your body. The warmth is pleasant. The sky is an ash grey. Before you, a large pool of lava appears.

Your humanoid replica appears on screen.

You need food, shelter, and drinking water.

Please select your initial path for exploration.

WereAllDoomed4000 has selected WALK FORWARD.

You step forward and tumble into the lava. Though you might scream, you cannot be heard. The molten lava sucks you down.

I'm sorry. You are dead.

Thank you for using the BetterEarth™ World Builder.

———

No information entered into the BetterEarth™ World Builder.

Global population update.

Previous estimate: 4

Current estimate: 0

Human extinction achieved!

Thank you for using the BetterEarth™ World Builder, please enter login credentials to continue.

BEYOND THE EDGE OF
THE HORIZON

1

NOTHING WAS THE SAME.

Everything, it seemed, was different.

The eyes. The fold of the skin about his neck.

And the wrinkles on his forehead.

All different.

Susanna sat back in the squishy armchair, the one which they'd inherited from Todd's parents. The *only* thing they'd inherited from Todd's parents. The armchair with the steel-blue fabric with the silvery stitching. A multitude of stains: mulchy browns—coffee?—to the light greys—perspiration? Beaten up. Lived in . . . or should that be *on*. And impossibly comfortable. The right balance between softness, of the pillows, and the rigidness, of its frame. The armchair seemed to carry with it an odour of sandalwood, that smell she recalled from the visits to Todd's father—to Toby—when he'd been living alone. All stuffed up in that old person's home for the last of his days. But he'd taken this armchair with him. And then, when he'd died, they'd taken it with them. Just thinking back to the home, to those visits, brought up memories of those bitter, watery soups the kitchens always insisted on serving. Along with those crusty bread rolls—the mouldy parts clearly picked off them by a careful kitchen assistant—and which she'd been sure were sourced from that broken-down, old bakery they would always pass on the corner, on the way to the car park.

As she sat back in the armchair, allowed herself to sink deeper into its cushions, she heard the unoiled *creak* of springs. She closed her eyes tight so she didn't have to see *him* anymore.

It made her feel better to sit here with her eyes shut.

Almost comforted her.

But not completely.

Nothing could comfort her completely now.

The timbre of Todd's voice was changed too. Before the tone had been lilting, and soft, but now it was all hardened up, like an orange peel leathered from being left out in the sun. He only spoke when spoken to . . . and then most reluctantly.

Monosyllabically.

And so she had pretty much given up speaking to him at all.

And those distant stares. The ones that seemed to hold onto her eyes—*just for a moment*—before drifting away, past her, into thin air, as if seeing something beyond that just wasn't there.

Or at least something she couldn't see.

And she knew, right now, if she opened her eyes, she'd see him staring—*staring* out of the bedroom window, out across the marsh-land. And out to the very shore of the lake.

The reeds would be swaying slightly in the breeze.

Caught up on the fine wind blowing down from the north.

A real winter's bite to the air now that they were in the clutches of autumn.

But she had no need to open her eyes to see that.

She just knew.

The question wasn't *what* Todd looked at, which was to say, *what* she saw herself. But it was, rather, just *what* it suggested to him. What he saw exactly in his own mind.

This lake house. The one they had bought so long ago—when they'd both been in their thirties and sick of their lives in the big city. Just after Todd had got the Big Promotion. Got himself involved in the Advanced Exploration Programme. When it had seemed the obvious thing to do. The thing they *should* do. Take the time to slow down. Swim in the butter-smooth waters, feel the fresh winds against their cheeks, and take long walks in the wild and pine-smelling forests.

That had been the plan.

A getaway.

A *perfect* getaway.

But now, now with Todd back, she couldn't help feel her heart wrench at the longing—the *wishing*—that someone, or something, would take him away.

Far away.

Because she was a prisoner here. Nothing more, nothing less. There were only mudflats for miles around. No other people. No other houses. No shops or anything of that nature.

Totally alone here, cast out into the wilderness.

But wasn't this just what she had wanted?

What they had *both* wanted?

2

PERHAPS SHE DOZED, or maybe her thinking just got the better of time, and she slipped away with it, but when she finally did open her eyes, it was to see Todd standing up there at the window. Just as she had pictured it, he was staring out over the lake. At the reeds.

At those *damn* swaying reeds.

His eyes were a clear blue, reflecting the grey, dimming twilight sky as it set in over the lake.

At this time of year the twilight was odd, as if it was a long, sustained moment, all wrapped up in a short period. Five, ten minutes. And then the night consumed it.

Ate it whole.

And it was gone again before the next day.

And the next . . . and the *next*.

Todd's lips were slightly parted as he stared. Often, as they'd sit like this, she would stare at the reflection off his eyes and believe she saw some sort of a film projecting right over them. Over their glossy surface. And she could see the players. And the scenes. All of them appearing out of Todd's subconscious. Leaping out from his memory. Held up bare to the dying light of the day.

Or maybe she was going mad.

As mad as Todd was.

Maybe *she* needed to get a grip on *herself*.

She took the first step, always the hardest, though it always fell to her. But, all the same, she knew that it needed taking. If no one took the step, then it might be a case of leaving Todd here all night. Staring out at that lake in the moonlight. Those stirring reeds set in an odd, effervescent glow in his irises. And he would be lost to her still. Just as he was lost to her now.

"Todd?" she said. "Todd?"

He remained at the window. Eyes still gleaming with the twilight—greyed-over sky.

"Todd?"

Still he didn't hear her. Or didn't *want* to hear her.

"You hungry?"

"Hmm?"

"I asked if you were hungry."

For a long, pregnant moment, he kept on staring out to the lake. Slowly, and with a seemingly infinite turning motion, he looked over his shoulder. But he didn't see her. He saw *through* her, and right to the sun-faded, beige flower-patterned wallpaper behind her. The wallpaper they'd always talked about stripping down and putting something a little 'jollier' up.

Or, at least, they'd discussed it before Todd had gone up on the mission.

Since he'd come back, they hadn't discussed it at all.

His cracked lips parted slightly and, in the final few seconds of daylight, she saw the tip of his tongue glistening with saliva. And the muscles in his throat contract and relax. The words seem to get stuck.

"You hungry?" she repeated again, as if this time he *would* hear it.

"Hmm?"

She felt the softness of the armchair beneath her. She wondered if she could stay here forever, or until the two of them: her and Todd, finally died. She was comfortable enough. Would it change anything really for her to get up, to go prepare a sandwich or whatever, and then marshal it down Todd's throat? . . . Or would it just all be for nothing—as it seemed to her now.

"I can make you something," she said.

Todd blinked once. Twice. A third time. And then, for the

fleetingest of moments, his eyes seemed to draw into focus. Those pale-blue eyes, the ones she'd fallen in love with the first time she'd seen him on that train—it seemed so long ago now—and that she hadn't been able to shake from her head till she'd seen him again, nearly a week later, and he'd asked her out for a coffee.

At some café nearby.

She couldn't remember its name, and, most likely, it'd got shut down by now.

Last time she'd been back to the city she'd hardly recognised the place—simply couldn't equate what was in her memory with what she saw with her eyes.

Was it the same for Todd now too?

Todd clasped his lips together and then gave her a subtle, but determined nod.

"Okay then," she said, rising up out of the chair, feeling the pins and needles in her bottom, and crawling their way through her thighs.

Her mouth tasted dry and stale, and she knew that she wasn't eating anywhere near enough. Just hadn't since the day Todd had left on the mission. She'd thought, when they got back, that things would be different. That she would find her appetite again. But, instead, she'd just felt worse.

She jabbed her toes into her slippers—into those warm, cream-coloured slippers that'd got all fuzzed up from the times she'd stuck them in the washing machine. 'Well-loved', that was what they were. Or that was how her mother would've put it.

She breathed in the sandalwood for the final time, savouring that familiar, comforting smell—the smell she'd breathed in over and over while she'd thought about Todd, up there, in space, edging closer to the extreme of mankind's knowledge, ready to bring back answers they had sought for so long. And he had brought back those answers. The answers had come back just fine.

But, Todd hadn't.

As she made her way out of the bedroom, along the bare wooden floorboards, and to the kitchen, she listened to the gentle *drip-drip* of raindrops falling on the roof tiles. The slight drop in temperature. The hairs rising up on her arms, and at the back of her neck.

The mouldy smell of rain as it rippled through the air.

And—for a moment—she recalled a time in her past.

In her and Todd's past.

When the two of them had gone out for the day on their bicycles, with a picnic basket—a bottle of white wine, cheese sandwiches—and how they'd got caught by the greying sky. And the falling night. And then it had rained on them. That night they'd taken shelter beneath a wise, old oak tree. And listened to the *patter* of the raindrops. And then to the dribble of the water through the leaves. The few raindrops which had fallen on her bare skin had been like little drops of life.

She would *never* forget that day.

Not for as long as she lived.

. . . And she wondered if Todd had already forgotten.

3

THE KITCHEN LIGHT bobbed its sallow glow over the dulled marble surfaces, and over the mahogany-fronted cabinets. It caught the knives with a gleam, and the cabinet handles too. It made the world outside invisible. That made her glad. What did she need the world outside for now?

What was it to her?

It no longer presented opportunity, or frontiers to be explored. It was what trapped her *inside*—in *here*—in this house, with her navel-gazing husband.

For the rest of eternity.

She looked over Todd, caught his blank gaze, and then reached out, felt for his muscular, hairy forearm, and guided him down onto one of the wicker kitchen chairs. She listened to it creak gently as it took his weight. Like always, his expression was neutral. His gaze still way out beyond. And his lips slightly parted. Could she take this for much longer?

Should she take this for much longer?

Or was she just wasting her life . . . because it was clear that Todd's was already gone.

She worked quickly, efficiently—*cleanly*—slicing up the tomatoes, and spreading the margarine, chopping the cheese. Before long, she had Todd's dinner, and hers, all ready to go. She laid it all on top of a porcelain plate with egg-shell blue edges, and then placed it before him. She took her own sandwich and sat across the table.

At first, she used to wait for Todd to begin eating, but she had learned that he took his time. Took his *own* sweet time to . . . how to put it? . . . *discover* his food—that was right. It was a glacial process, and one which tied her gut up in knots. Some nights she became almost certain that he wouldn't eat at all. That he would simply gaze off into mid-air until he finally starved to death. More and more, she had got to wondering whether that might be a mercy for both of them.

Wasn't it better to live a widow, than to walk the Earth holding hands with the dead?

Or was that just more of that 'unconstructive thinking' that her therapist was always going on about—and which *he* seemed to believe was the bane of her life.

She had always been practical. Plain speaking. Surely that had been one of the reasons that Todd had married her in the first place.

Wouldn't he be . . . *wasn't* he, locked away somewhere inside there, disappointed that she had sacrificed herself like she had for him?

Turned her life into a half-life?

There was no way of knowing until Todd spoke. So, she guessed, until then, she could make up just whatever she wanted to believe. And it would turn out just fine.

At the base of her mind, though, she knew for certain that she *had* to know the answer. No matter how painful. And she *had* to make the call.

The call she had been so afraid to make for all these weeks.

Because of what it might mean.

But she knew that she had to make it all the same.

Else she would never know.

If there was one thing she couldn't face, it was dying without knowing.

4

S USANNA WAITED till Todd had finished his sandwich
and then put him to bed. As always, he seemed indifferent to
the idea. Not at all interested in the disrobing process. In getting
into his light-blue silk pyjamas with his name stitched in gold
thread across the breast pocket, the ones she'd bought for his
return. The ones she'd thought might be fitting for a hero.

She helped him in between the sheets of their shared bed. And
she drew the blinds on the night. On the bright Moon which
beamed down over the lake. If she didn't then she was likely to
return to the bedroom, and to see him standing there, eyes fixed
looking out the window, just staring into the water. And though
she couldn't be certain he would sleep, she could at least be certain
that, with the blinds drawn, and complete darkness settling on the
bedroom, he would stay where he was.

Eyes wide open. Staring up at the ceiling.

But he would stay.

Back in the kitchen, she flipped through her notebook, the one
she had stuffed to the back of the drawer. The one that she had
hardly thought for a second about when she'd withdrawn it from
her handbag the day Todd's ship had set down.

The day he had returned.

She still recalled the dusky smell to the air, the thick dust
puffing up, the sun beaming down hard on everyone. The middle
of a scorching afternoon. No better day to return to Earth with
a *bump*.

She had been so nervous. She'd chewed her way through a
whole packet of peppermint gum in the hope of getting shot of that
bloody warm taste in her mouth. The one she'd tasted for most of
the week leading up to Todd's arrival. The one she tasted now,

252

flipping through the curled pages of the notebook. All that warmth as she'd waited in the sunlight, and then she'd seen his ship coming down—*flying* down out of the atmosphere.

At first like a star peeping through the blue sky.

And then like a plummeting comet.

And, finally, just like an aeroplane.

An ordinary, everyday aeroplane.

Nothing had thrown her off. Nothing had turned her attention away. And nothing had made an impact on her until she'd heard that *screech* of the rubber tyres making contact with the ink-black asphalt. And that puff of smoke coming up from the surface.

That was when she'd felt odd. Something within her—something intrinsic, and yet totally persuasive—told her that there was a problem.

Though she couldn't have said what it was.

And then the chatter of the people around her had re-entered her hearing. And then she had watched the spaceship come to a halt. And the door open. And the men . . . *two* of them, peek out into the glimmering sunlight. And Todd hadn't been one of them.

That was when she had felt the prickle up her spine, another sign that she had been correct.

That her assumption had been correct.

That something had gone *terribly* wrong.

She'd watched the two crewmembers return to the spaceship, help Todd out, take him along behind them, to the top of the steps. Lead him down as if he was a little old maid.

And she'd felt her stomach dip, and her heart leap to her mouth.

But she'd reasoned with herself. Tried to stop herself becoming too worried. It couldn't be as bad as it looked. It was *never* as bad as it looked. That was the mantra she had lived her life by—the one which had stood her in good stead, right till now.

It was the one that was going to be most challenged in the coming months. That still *was* being challenged to this day.

All she had wanted to do, when she had managed to prise her way through the crowd, away from the rest of the audience, and to the astronauts, was touch him. Touch Todd's face. Run her hands through his thinning blond hair, and press her lips to those cracked, adventurer's lips of his. But they had held her back.

The medics had looked at him. And found nothing wrong.

She had felt the relief lift from her shoulders. The muscles unknot themselves. And her heart find a steady equilibrium.

How *false* that relief had been.

And yet how tempting.

Only when she and Todd had been on the point of leaving, and one of Todd's crewmates had demanded that she take his phone number down, just in case she wanted to speak, had the implication of the thing come back to her.

The other crewmate had watched on from a distance. Clearly not wishing to become involved. And then she had driven them both—herself and Todd—right back here.

Back home.

She had been so sure that it was the right thing to do.

The *only* thing to do.

And that she was the *only* one to do it.

Now, though, she saw that she needed help.

She found the page with the crewmate's number on:

Ronald Peason.

THICK, HONEY-SMOOTH ringing tones sounded in her ear. It had been a long time since she had phoned anybody. Not since Todd was back at least. Both her parents were dead. Her relatives were all dead. And she had no friends. She guessed she either tired people—or she grew tired of them. But the result was the same.

She sat on the rigid, wicker kitchen chair and stared out into the blackness. There were no curtains in the kitchen. Only the great big sliding doors which glared back at her. Splashing her reflection back. In the shadowy reflection, she could make out her neat, cropped blond hair. Her spindly limbs. The ones which'd won her so many medals—so many sporting honours in her adolescence. And which had grown frailer, weedier, *spindlier* over the years. And though she could easily make out her entire body in the reflection, she couldn't see her face for the shadow cast over it. Making her seem almost detached from her own body.

She waited for what seemed like hours, with the heel of her hand propping her head up on the table, her other hand pressing the plastic handset to her ear. That same ringing tone in her head, nuzzling her inner ear, before she heard the *click* at the other end, and the unsteady, sleep-bleary, "Hello?"

She swallowed hard. Still tasting pieces of cheese between her teeth—feeling a light draught eek its way about the kitchen floor. Nipping at her bare ankles. "This is Todd's wife. Susanna."

"Susanna?" the voice replied—*Ronald Peason* replied. "Do you . . . I mean, what time is it there, with you?"

She hadn't thought about time. She hadn't thought about time for a *long* while. But now she did, she remembered the large, chunky, oak-wood kitchen clock which hung above her head. She eyed its thick, gently moving hands as they ticked along.

Nine o'clock.

At least here.

Where was Ronald living?

Where did he live?

She thought it over a moment, and then realised that—really—she didn't care all that much. She had rung for one reason, and one reason only. Once she had her answer she would hang up, and they wouldn't speak again. "It's about Todd," she said, feeling her voice quiver a touch. "What . . . what happened to him?"

Heavy breathing on the other end. Then a hard exhale, as if the answer would take some extremely weighty words indeed. And, for all she knew, it would.

Because she knew nothing.

"How much did he tell you about the mission?"

"He told me some. All that he was *allowed* to let me know."

"Hmm."

She glanced off into the darkened corridor. To the bedroom. For a second she was convinced she saw Todd's silhouette. Todd staring out from the darkness at her. She fantasied about his charming smile . . . the one he had used to charm her.

But she knew that was impossible.

The Todd she'd known was gone now.

And, in any case, there was no one there.

"Listen," Ronald said, "I couldn't, you know, call you back a little later, uh, I mean, *earlier?* You know it's past midnight out here, and I've gotta get up with the kids in a little while. They don't sleep all that much. Not at this age."

Susanna felt her throat tighten. Her pulse quickened. She thought about how long she had put off this call. And how much accumulated energy it had taken her to finally make it.

Would she ever be able to do it again?

Could she spend another night lying in bed beside Todd while he stared up at the ceiling? . . . She could *only* lie since she believed it impossible for *any*one to sleep beside someone who lay on their back with their eyes wrenched open.

Just staring.

Staring all the time.

"I . . . I, ah," Susanna started, "if it's all the same with you—if you don't mind *terribly*—then I'd prefer to speak about it now. You see, uh, things have got worse. Or, well, at least I think they have."

More heavy breathing. Perhaps a low female voice in the background.

Ronald's wife?

A little further off, there was the sound of crying.

A child crying?

Had she done that with her phone call? Had her ringing at this time meant that she'd shaken up the routine of the house— Ronald's house—turned everything on its head, stirred up the coals and got the flames raging? It really didn't matter. Because she *had* to know right now.

Some answer. *An* answer.

On the other end of the line, she heard the *squeak* of bedsprings—the *rustle* of a bed sheet being thrown off. And then footsteps. The gentle *creak* of floorboards beneath feet. She pictured Ronald, telephone stuck to his ear, making his way to some quiet nook. A dark place, she hoped. There was always something more intimate about speaking on the phone with the darkness all around.

Another sigh, and the squeaking of yet more springs. She imagined that Ronald had found himself a chair. "Hello?" he said. "I can speak now."

She listened hard. To the slight *patter* of raindrops on the roof tiles of the lake house. To the gentle *purr* of the central heating kicking in. And to the gentle sweep of the draught blowing in beneath the door.

When Ronald spoke again, his voice was weary, but not pissed off—at least not how she might've imagined. After all she *had* woken him up in the middle of the night. Everything about his tone suggested expectation. He had been expecting this conversation for a long time.

Just as she had.

"You've got nothing else out of him, then?" Ronald said.

"No."

"And you've, uh, not taken up any offers for professional help, you know, it might be worth thinking—"

"No," Susanna said, her voice much sharper than she'd expected. When she spoke again, she made a point to soften up, just a little. "No, I wanted to work it out for myself. It's just . . . well, I guess I've thought this whole time—the whole time since he's been back, that perhaps, just *perhaps*—he might spring a crack in his shell, you know, like snap back to his senses all of a sudden?"

"Hmm."

"Please, don't say that."

"Say what?"

"I . . . I mean, I'm sorry—I didn't mean to be impolite. It's just, you sound like him when you answer like that."

"Like what?"

"You know, just *hum* in agreement."

"Oh, I see," Ronald said, "I'm sorry."

Again, there wasn't any trace of a scolding tone. Nothing whatsoever. Just the slight weariness of a conversation long expected, and, in many ways, already suffered through in its antic-ipation.

"Really," Susanna said. "It doesn't matter, I . . . I don't know—I was just being silly. Sometimes I get too sensitive. Maybe it's just cabin fever." She tried a chuckle but it died in her throat. "You know what I mean?"

". . . *Yes*," Ronald said, pointedly this time.

Susanna just sat still. Impossibly still. It felt like she was in a nurse's office. Ready to get a vaccination, or to have her blood drawn for a test. She felt that same icy chill. The thing that she'd dreaded for so long, built up into a great ominous mountain in her mind was finally about to enter her everyday reality. And, like the mountain, there was simply nothing she could do to stop it.

"I'm ready," she said.

6

I N THE DISTANCE, on Ronald's end of the phone line, Susanna heard the raggedy sobs of a baby, and she heard the *creak* of the springs, or the wooden frame of the chair he was sitting on. As he turned to look. To see if there was anything for him to do.

For a terrifying moment, she was certain he had forgotten the question. That he had lost the thread of their conversation in his half-awake state. But then he spoke. And removed the doubt from her mind. Eased her worries of having to ask him for a second time.

He started with a long-suppressed sigh. "Nothing about the mission was easy—I've got to tell you that right now. Not one of us came back the same man as before. That's the other thing you've got to bear in mind."

Sure, she knew that. How else could it be? They'd been gone for five years. Testing the latest innovation in spaceship design. Going right to the fringe of the visible universe. Going to see just *what* was out there. *Pushing* the limits of just what mankind thought was possible. She knew that. That was what she'd signed up to the day that she'd married Todd. She *understood*.

What she hadn't understood, it dawned on her now, was how much scope there could've been for Todd to change. It was one thing for him to go away—the cocksure, action hero he had been . . . and then to come back as . . . as, well, there was no other way to put it:

To come back as a *husk*.

Another sigh on Ronald's end of the line. "No, we've all changed—it was impossible for us not to change. I'd be first to admit it was Todd that changed the most, though. I mean, me and Daniel, well, we stood up fine. Remained, uh . . . *functional* throughout the mission. Though it coulda just as easily have been one of us that came back . . . well, you know, the way Todd came back."

She breathed in deep. Felt the prickle of air about her lungs. Blood flowing up to her head. Making her feel more awake, and dizzier, in equal measure. She had to know. And she had to know *now*. "What did you see there? What did you see beyond the edge of the horizon?"

A long pause. No breathing. No other sounds. For a moment she was certain the line had been cut. A slight panic beat on her brow, and she stared into that endless reflection in the sliding doors opposite her. At her own body. Out here. In the wilderness. *Alone*.

"Nothing," Ronald said finally. "I mean, we found nothing special. Nothing we didn't *expect* to find."

"Wh . . . what do you mean?"

"I mean what I said," he replied, for the first time sounding impatient. "We *saw* nothing. Nothing at all. Just more space. *Yet more* space. There was nothing special. Just like we thought, and—"

"But, I . . . I don't understand. In that case what happened to Todd. What's . . . what's"—she felt her throat tighten—"what's *wrong* with him?"

"I wish I knew, Susanna, but I really can't say. We, well, when we reached the point, slipped past the visible universe, I noticed some change come over Todd. Something about his whole pose. He just, well, I don't know any other way to put it . . . he just *slumped*. Like someone dug a valve into his lungs and depressed the air right out of him."

"I . . . I see."

"Yeah, I remember noticing it fine at the time. Didn't think to mention it to Daniel till later, though, when Todd wouldn't answer none of our questions. Wouldn't make so much as a peep. Then we both saw the change in him, the . . . the change that'd come over him."

"But, . . . *why?*"

"Listen, Susanna, I think Todd needs professional help. I think, without being too meddling, that now's the time to look into it. Really. I'm no expert, nothing like that, but you're best off trying to help him as soon as possible. To see . . . to see, well, to see if he can't be *saved*."

'Saved'. Yes. That was what Todd needed now. She knew it. But *how?*

Was it just like Ronald said. Did he just need to go see some *professional*. Would they *really* find a solution to the problem—have a shot at bringing Todd back?

Well, she supposed she could try.

If she could bring herself to leave the lake house. To head out with him. And for the two of them to head back to the city. She supposed she could do it that way.

As the thoughts skittered about her head, she recalled that Ronald was still on the other end. Still hanging on the phone. "I . . . ah, I mean, there's *nothing* then? Nothing you can add to it. Nothing you can think that might've, you know, triggered the thing."

"Like I said, the *thing* was immediate. Like clicking your fingers. And he was gone. Almost like, well, like someone had given him a shove off into space, then watched him float away."

"Like . . . lobotomised?"

"I didn't want to put it so bluntly—"

"No, that's fine. That's just fine. I guess for all this time now, for all these weeks, I've just been lying to myself, you know, pulling wool down over my eyes. The whole time I should've been thinking about what's best for Todd. Thinking about what he needs to get better."

"Sure, sure—I guess it's an overwhelming time."

"You could say that."

A pause thickened between them. Dead air. Only the gentle buzz of the phone line reminding her there was another person on the other end, then Ronald said, "Listen, Susanna, you know, feel free to call any time you want, though . . . well, I'd appreciate it if you called a little later on"—he stopped briefly, and checked his tone, brightening up several degrees, or at least it seemed that way to Susanna's ear—"Might catch me being more awake and all, that'd be a bonus, eh?"

"Sure. I'm sorry for waking you. It's just, well, I don't know, it just seemed urgent, that's all."

"Sure, sure, I understand. Totally understand." He yawned hard into the phone, and Susanna was certain she heard a mutter—Ronald's wife—maybe trying to coax him back to sleep; to get him back to sleep while he still could . . . before his baby woke them up again. "You call any time," he said. "Any time you need to talk. And . . ." his words faded off and Susanna was sure that he wasn't going to pick up the slack, he was going to leave the words unspoken, but then he continued ". . . say hi to Todd from me, would you? You know, just for what it's worth. Tell him, aw, tell him I *miss* him. And Danny does too, though he'd never come out and say it. Say hi to him from the both of us, okay?"

"Okay," Susanna said, and then the line went dead.

7

SUSANNA STARED at her darkened, silvery, shadowy reflection in the sliding doors. She peered out at the impenetrable night beyond. It'd been one of their rules, early on, when they'd first bought the lake house, that they'd never put up exterior lights.

So they could see the sky.

So they could see the *stars*.

She recalled, back before Todd had gone off on the mission, that the two of them would take the rumpled, plaid blankets out from the shed—the ones that smelled of damp earth—and spread them out just after twilight had tailed off. After the mosquitoes had gone to bed.

They'd just lie back, a few inches separating them, and they'd both stare upward into that midnight-blue fabric. Neither of them would talk. But that was fine.

It was just fine.

They'd only come back in when their lips began to shudder. When their teeth began to chatter. When Susanna could feel her face going numb. And her tongue turning to ice.

While Todd had been away, she'd often fantasised about what it might be like to simply lie out by the side of the lake till morning.

To feel the kiss of the early-morning dew.

To feel the frost webbing over her skin.

But she'd never tried it.

Never wanted to try it after Todd had shot off into space.

Lying out there, on the bank of the lake, had just reminded her of him.

And those reminders were painful.

Just about as painful as they were now.

Maybe it was minutes, or maybe it was hours later, but she eventually got up from the wicker chair, and trudged in a daze back through the house. Back to the bedroom. She made out Todd's form, traced by the drape of the bed sheets. And she made out the soft sparkle of his eyes. The slight trickle of moonlight getting in around the drapes bringing that sparkle out.

She lay down beside him. Felt the warmth of his body beside hers. Smelled that sandalwood from the armchair at the side of the bed. And thought back to their old life . . . what life had been like before he had gone away.

Just as she was drifting off to sleep, thinking up who she might dial up to help with Todd, who might be able to help her out with him . . . maybe even bring him back . . . she noticed him stir slightly —noticed him turn on his side to face her.

At first she was certain it was a dream, and—*goodness*—she'd had enough of those, but then she started to believe it was real. That he was *looking* right at her. With two very *conscious* eyes.

"You know what I saw?" he asked.

The air went crisp in her throat, and she just about managed to prise the words out between her lips. ". . . Uh, no, what?"

"I saw us," he said. "*Us* projected right back. Silver shadows."

She felt her eyes bob all over his, and a prickling sensation pass about her skull.

"Yeah, that's right," he said. "Just like ghosts. Ghosts looking back at *us*."

She didn't dare speak. Afraid that her words might shatter him. Somehow send him back into his shell. Send him scurrying back. But then she realised he had nothing left to say. *This* was what had been on his mind all the while. What had kept him away from her. Turned inward on himself.

In the darkness, she reached out and felt for his forearm. Felt those muscles rippling like steel cables. And she held on tight. Ever so gently—at first with just the brush of his fingertips—he draped his hand over hers.

They stayed that way till dawn.

AUTHOR'S NOTE

Thank you for taking the time to read one of my books. If you would like to hear about my latest releases you can sign up for my newsletter here: www.raymondsflex.com

Thanks for reading!

Raymond S Flex

Collected Science Fiction Short Stories
Volume One

Copyright © Raymond S Flex, 2016.
Published by DIB Books
All rights reserved.

Cover design and layout copyright © DIB Books, 2016.
Cover art copyright © Diversepixel / Shutterstock, 2014.